Zoos

Look for these and other books in the Lucent Overview Series:

Abortion	Illiteracy
Acid Rain	Immigration
AIDS	Money
Alcoholism	Ocean Pollution
Animal Rights	Oil Spills
The Beginning of Writing	The Olympic Games
Cancer	Organ Transplants
Child Abuse	Ozone
Cities	Pesticides
The Collapse of the Soviet Union	Police Brutality
Dealing with Death	Population
Death Penalty	Prisons
Democracy	Rainforests
Drugs and Sports	Recycling
Drug Trafficking	The Reunification of Germany
Eating Disorders	Smoking
Endangered Species	Space Exploration
Energy Alternatives	Special Effects in the Movies
Espionage	Teen Alcoholism
Extraterrestrial Life	Teen Pregnancy
Gangs	Teen Suicide
Garbage	The UFO Challenge
The Greenhouse Effect	The United Nations
Gun Control	The U.S. Congress
Hate Groups	Vanishing Wetlands
Hazardous Waste	Vietnam
The Holocaust	World Hunger
Homeless Children	Zoos

Zoos

by Diane Yancey

Library of Congress Cataloging-in-Publication Data

Yancey, Diane.
  Zoos / by Diane Yancey.
      p.   cm. — (Lucent overview series)
  Includes bibliographical references (p.   ) and index.
  ISBN 1-56006-163-4 (acid free paper)
  1. Zoos—Juvenile literature.   2. Animal rights—Juvenile
literature.   3. Endangered species—Juvenile literature.   4. Wildlife
conservation—Juvenile literature.   [1. Zoos. 2. Animal rights.
3. Wildlife conservation.]   I. Title.   II. Series.
  QL76.Y35   1994
  590'.74'4—dc20   94-8546
                                                                   CIP
                                                                    AC

No part of this book may be reproduced or used in any form or by any means, electrical, mechanical, or otherwise, including, but not limited to, photocopy, recording, or any information storage and retrieval system, without prior written permission from the publisher.

Copyright © 1995 by Lucent Books, Inc.
P.O. Box 289011, San Diego, CA 92198-9011
Printed in the U.S.A.

Contents

INTRODUCTION	7
CHAPTER ONE An Exotic History	11
CHAPTER TWO A New Breed of Zoo	27
CHAPTER THREE Problem Zoos	45
CHAPTER FOUR Do We Have the Right?	59
CHAPTER FIVE Zoos as Arks	77
CHAPTER SIX Zoos for Tomorrow	95
GLOSSARY	109
ORGANIZATIONS TO CONTACT	113
SUGGESTIONS FOR FURTHER READING	116
WORKS CONSULTED	117
INDEX	121
ABOUT THE AUTHOR	127
PICTURE CREDITS	128

Introduction

EVERY YEAR MORE than 350 million people visit zoos throughout the world. Adults and children alike stream through entry gates to gawk at gorillas, peer at polar bears, and fill up on popcorn and cold drinks. In the United States, the number of visitors to zoos in one year—more than 100 million—is greater than the combined annual attendance at all major-league baseball, football, and basketball games.

A trip to the zoo is one of the most traditional forms of entertainment today. Although zoos do seek to entertain, they have more important functions as well. They are excellent sources of education, places to gain a greater understanding of nature and the environment. More importantly, they are sanctuaries for untold numbers of endangered animals.

One example of this kind of animal haven is the International Wildlife Conservation Park, commonly known as the Bronx Zoo. One of five zoos in New York City, the Bronx Zoo is managed by the New York Zoological Society, lately renamed NYZS/Wildlife Conservation Society.

Visitors to the Bronx Zoo enjoy exploring its many fine exhibits. Jungle World is a miniature Asian forest, where artificial rain falls every day on a tangle of exotic vines, shrubs, and ferns.

(Opposite page) Visitors watch keepers bathe African elephants at the Pittsburgh Zoo. In addition to providing entertainment for more than 350 million visitors annually, modern zoos also serve as educators for the public and as sanctuaries for endangered animals.

A fence enables visitors to get a close but protected view of a Siberian tiger at the Bronx Zoo. Some people question whether animals should be removed from their natural habitat and displayed in zoos.

Monkeys chatter overhead. Leopards, turtles, and other wildlife live much as they would in the wild. The Himalayan Highlands exhibit allows zoogoers to walk through a "natural" mountain landscape and to catch glimpses of red pandas and snow leopards. In the children's zoo, youngsters go hands-on with a giant spider web, crawl into a kid-sized snail shell, and explore model prairie dog tunnels.

Although zoos—short for zoological gardens—are one of the best ways to teach people about wildlife, not all zoos do this very well. The late Slater Park Zoo in Pawtucket, Rhode Island, is an example of a facility that fell short both in educating visitors and in caring for its animals.

For years, Slater Park Zoo was a reasonably attractive zoo that entertained about 100,000 visitors a year. Its grounds were clean. Its animals appeared healthy. A baby animal born every so often seemed to indicate that all was well.

Still, to the critical eye, Slater Park Zoo failed to measure up. Instead of a balanced diet, animals were reportedly fed chips and soda from the park concession stands. Several animals had allegedly died as a result of overcrowding in recent years. The zoo's forty-year-old elephant had spent most of her life in solitary confinement even though elephants in the wild normally move in herds.

Suffering from a shortage of funds, Slater Park Zoo went out of business in 1993, but zoos with similar shortcomings continue to operate. Most people agree that such zoos are a problem and do not deserve to remain open. Others go one step further. They hold the belief that wild animals belong in the wild and should never be held in zoos, no matter how well run. They believe that it would be far better to eliminate the practice of caging animals altogether and work to protect them in their natural surroundings.

Modern zoos feature exhibits designed to resemble the natural habitats of the animals. In the miniature rain forest of the Jungle World exhibit at the Bronx Zoo, animals live in a nearly natural setting.

In the words of ecologists David Phillips and Sandra Kaiser:

> [The roles of zoos] are being increasingly challenged. . . . More and more people are coming to believe that animals have a right to exist in their own natural habitats, instead of being shown off for the amusement of humans.

The fate of zoos depends on how these challenges are handled. People must decide if zoos can be justified in our world today, if humankind has the right to deprive wild animals of their freedom, and if it is practical to spend money on artificial habitats rather than on natural environments. For zoos to survive, they must demonstrate that their efforts to preserve wildlife are unique and invaluable. They must continue to deal with issues ranging from species selection to funding, while meeting new challenges in the wild that include mass extinction and genetic inbreeding.

Whether zoos will prove essential to our world is a question remaining to be answered by an increasingly critical society. Without wisdom and a great deal of foresight, zoos may become one more example of how people meddle with and mismanage their world in spite of the best of intentions.

1

An Exotic History

ACCORDING TO SOME historians, the first zoo was created thousands of years ago when Noah gathered animals into the ark, protecting them from a flood that threatened to destroy all life on earth. Bible scholars believe that this floating menagerie included two of every species living at the time, estimated to be about 45,000 animals, not including fish or insects.

Real zoos, permanent collections of animals, came into existence many years after Noah. With the appearance of cities and royalty, humans had the time and desire to create zoos. Made up of unique creatures from foreign lands, these zoos were not arks. They did nothing to save animals. Instead, they merely displayed the importance and power of the rulers who established them.

Power and status

In ancient times, collecting animals was often a sideline of war. Triumphant warriors presented their monarchs with trophies—slaves, treasure, and unusual animals—on their return to the homeland. About 1500 B.C., Egyptian queen Hatshepsut was the first known ruler to send out expeditions specifically for capturing animals. Ships to southern Africa reportedly returned with such exotic creatures as greyhound dogs, monkeys, and giraffes.

(Opposite page) According to the Bible, Noah gathered two of every animal species into his ark, protecting them from a flood that threatened to destroy all life on earth. Today, zoos are often referred to as arks for their role as protectors of endangered species.

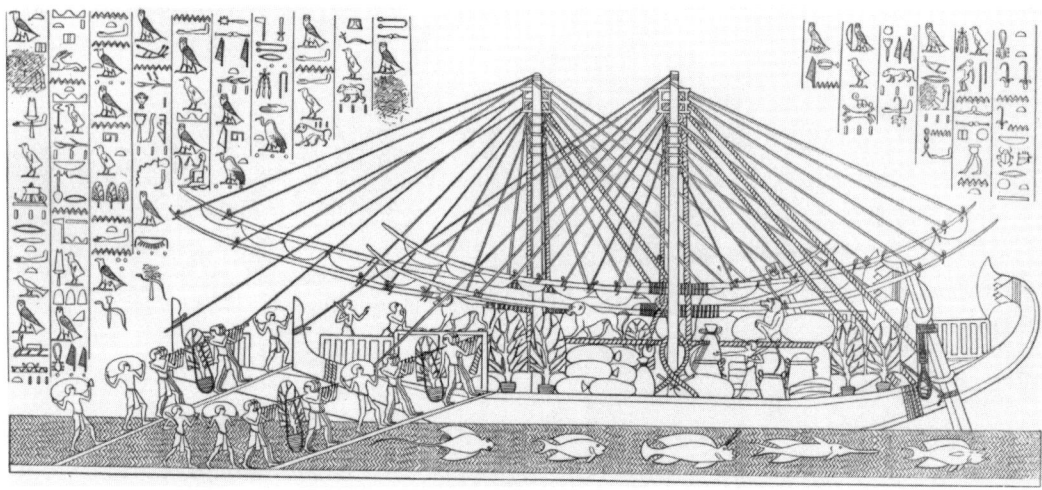

An engraving, dated about 1500 B.C., depicts the loading of an ancient Egyptian ship. The Egyptians were the first known people to send out expeditions for the purpose of capturing exotic animals.

Giraffes were a popular exhibit of Egyptian royalty. King Ramses II had several in his menagerie around 1250 B.C. So did King Ptolemy II. Also found in Ptolemy's impressive collection were cheetahs, lions, and possibly the first chimpanzees to be brought into captivity. History records a huge animal parade organized by the king that included thousands of birds—ostriches, peacocks, parrots, and pheasants—plus dozens of elephants, lions, camels, snakes, and a rhinoceros.

Eastern and Middle Eastern zoos

Other early Middle Eastern "zookeepers" were Ashurbanipal, king of Assyria, and Nebuchadnezzar, king of Babylon. According to history, Nebuchadnezzar specialized in collecting lions. King Solomon, the Hebrew ruler famous for his wealth and wisdom, collected apes, deer, exotic birds, and horses from many countries during his reign in about 950 B.C.

Rulers in Asia also set up several impressive zoos. Emperor Wen Wang's "Garden of Intelligence," established about 1000 B.C. in China, covered fifteen hundred acres. Details of the zoo are sketchy, but the collection was made up of animals from the entire kingdom of China, including a giant panda. Apparently this animal was as unique and prized an exhibit then as it is today.

During his visit to the East about A.D. 1270, explorer Marco Polo discovered the zoo of Mongol emperor Kublai Khan. The emperor's menagerie contained a variety of animals, from hippos to bears, and porcupines to monkeys. Kublai Khan was said to need more than one hundred people just to handle his enormous collection of hawks and falcons.

Educate and entertain

Although most early zoos were founded exclusively for the enjoyment of the nobility, some exceptions did exist. They are considered the forerunners of public zoos.

By about 300 B.C., many Greek city-states kept collections of exotic animals. These collections formed a part of the education of young intellectuals. The great teacher and philosopher Aristotle most likely benefited from this system of education. His book *History of Animals*, in which he described hundreds of species in great detail, was a result of his study of exotic animals found in Greek zoos.

Akbar, emperor of the Mogul Empire, established public zoos in many cities across India during his reign in the late 1500s. Akbar's zoos were stocked with a wide variety of exotic beasts, including lions, tigers, rhinos, elephants, and camels. Specially trained veterinarians watched over the animals' health and well-being.

Akbar was especially fascinated with the cheetah, the fastest land animal known to humans. The ruler kept almost one thousand of the big cats in a royal menagerie at his palace. When they failed to breed, he opened the royal grounds to them. Akbar believed, correctly, that if the cheetahs had

Akbar, sixteenth-century emperor of the Mogul Empire, appointed specially trained veterinarians to watch over the health and well-being of his many exotic zoo animals.

more room to roam, they would be happier and more likely to reproduce. In spite of his efforts, however, the animals produced only one litter.

Modern zookeepers have also discovered the difficulty of breeding cheetahs. More than three centuries passed before another litter was born in captivity. That event took place in the Philadelphia Zoo in 1956.

Misunderstood and mistreated

Under the protection of these early rulers, animals in zoos probably lived more pampered lives than did ordinary human beings. Yet, unlike Akbar, other royals often did not understand the needs of the exotic creatures. For instance, King Ptolemy II did not know that his chimpanzees could easily catch many human diseases. The chimps probably did not live long, in spite of the tender care they received.

Although royalty prized their animals, they were also guilty of mistreating them. The practice of animal baiting, putting animals together to watch them fight, was popular with royals and common people alike. Many zoos had baiting arenas. Often this was the only part of royal zoos in which the public was allowed.

The practice of collecting animals for fighting reached a bloody peak during the Roman Empire. Not all animals in Roman zoos at this time were destined for the arenas, but, as historian W.E.H. Lecky records:

> In a single day, at the dedication of the Colosseum by Titus, five thousand animals perished. Under Trajan, the games continued for one hundred and twenty-three successive days. Lions, tigers, elephants, rhinoceroses, hippopotami, giraffes, bulls, stags, even crocodiles and serpents were employed to give novelty to the spectacle.

Royal menageries had to be enormous to make this sort of sacrifice possible.

With the fall of the Roman Empire around A.D. 470, zoos in Europe almost disappeared. Not until after Christopher Columbus's momentous journey to the New World in 1492 did European nobility again take an interest in collecting animals. On his return to Spain, Columbus described the unusual creatures he found in the West Indies, among them iguanas, macaws, and various other tropical birds. His tales inspired later expeditions to look for New World animals that could enhance European zoos.

Spanish explorer Hernando Cortés was unprepared for the impressive royal zoo he and his men discovered when they came upon the Aztec civilization in Central America about 1520. Set on an island, the capital city of Tenochtitlán was ornamented with aviaries of brightly colored birds.

Animal baiting, putting animals together to watch them fight, once was a popular form of entertainment. An illustration depicts elephant baiting in India.

Outside the city, King Montezuma's royal zoo included cougars and jaguars housed in bronze cages. There were colorful fish in large, well-kept ponds, giant turtles, rattlesnakes, bears, sloths, and armadillos. Montezuma, an excellent zoo director, engaged hundreds of keepers and veterinarians to care for his enormous menagerie.

Cortés spared little thought for the zoo when he laid siege to the capital in 1521. The city's starving residents ate most of the animals to survive. The conquistadors later completed the zoo's destruction when they leveled the city and set fire to the aviaries.

Zoos go public

After the 1500s, new species from the Americas added interest and variety to a growing number of royal zoos in Europe. King Louis XIII of

An artist depicts Christopher Columbus, startled by an iguana in the West Indies. His tales of exotic animals inspired later animal-collecting expeditions to the New World.

France was one of the first to display American animals. In 1624, he established a zoo in Versailles, France, that included tapirs (hoglike mammals related to the rhinoceros), condors, hummingbirds, lemurs (large-eyed relations of the monkey), and birds of paradise.

Other proud members of royalty soon displayed New World turkeys, llamas, and guinea pigs for the first time. By the 1700s, such exotic species as penguins, emus, kangaroos, raccoons, and South American monkeys had been imported to Europe.

European zoos soon began to change in another way. In 1765, Holy Roman emperor Joseph II opened the Schönbrunn Zoo in Vienna, Austria, to the public. Joseph's father, Francis I, had earlier presented this royal menagerie to his wife, Maria Theresa, as a unique birthday present. The zoo included twelve animal houses circled around a garden pavilion where the empress ate breakfast on sunny days. The Schönbrunn Zoo was later modernized and still operates today. It is recognized as the oldest surviving zoo in the world.

Throughout the seventeenth and eighteenth centuries many expeditions were undertaken in search of exotic species that could enhance the growing number of royal zoos in Europe.

An illustration depicts the grand opening of the Elephant House at Regent's Park Zoo. Regent's Park Zoo was a member of the Zoological Society of London, the first society of its kind.

In the 1790s, the French Revolution eliminated the positions of king, queen, and other nobility in France. Shortly after that, the Royal Gardens in Paris, stocked with many of the animals formerly in the royal zoo at Versailles, opened to the public.

In 1844, King Frederick William IV of Prussia donated his private animal collection to the German people, marking the beginning of the present-day Zoologischer Garten Berlin (Berlin Zoo).

Zoological societies

As private menageries opened and the public got its first look at exotic animals, the demand for zoos grew. Still, royalty could not be relied on to satisfy this demand. As a result, zoological societies were formed, made up of wealthy and enthusiastic individuals who believed that establishing and supporting a good zoo was worth the cost.

The Zoological Society of London was the first to be created, in 1826. The idea originated with Sir Thomas Stamford Raffles, an energetic and creative businessman. With the help of a friend, Sir Joseph Banks, Raffles defined the aims of the new society. They included "the advancement of zoology and animal physiology, and the introduction of new and curious subjects of the animal kingdom." The Regent's Park Zoo, founded by Raffles and located in London's Regent's Park, opened in 1828.

Sometime later, the idea of zoological societies spread to the United States. The Philadelphia Zoological Society was the first to be formed, in 1859. Actual creation of the Philadelphia Zoo had to wait until the close of the Civil War. The zoo opened its gates in 1874.

U.S. zoos

New York City's Central Park Zoo (renamed the Central Park Wildlife Conservation Center in 1993) opened in 1864 and was recognized as the first zoo in the United States. The Bronx Zoo (International Wildlife Conservation Park) opened in 1899, shortly after the formation of the city's zoological society.

Other large American cities also established zoos in the late 1800s. The Buffalo Zoo in New York State was created in 1870. Chicago's Lincoln Park Zoo opened about the same time, followed by zoos in Cincinnati, Baltimore, and Cleveland. In 1889 Congress established the National Zoological Park in Washington, D.C. This government-funded facility, commonly known as the National Zoo, is associated with the Smithsonian Institution.

Pleasing the visitor

By the late 1800s, the age of public zoos had arrived. Ordinary people regularly turned out dressed in their Sunday best to ride elephants, laugh at the monkeys, and watch keepers poke meat through the bars of the lion cages.

In these so-called modern zoos, animals were grouped by family. Old World monkeys were placed next to their New World relatives. American cougars lived next to African lions and Indian tigers.

Most animals were kept indoors, in buildings that could be artificially heated when winters got too cold. These buildings, with generic titles such as the Lion House or the Giraffe House, were often copies of human architecture. Little thought was given to reproducing the natural habitat of the animal. In Germany, the Zebra House at the Berlin Zoo was Arabian in style. The Düsseldorf Zoo housed its Barbary sheep in what appeared to be a ruined castle. At Regent's Park Zoo in London, the Camel House resembled a brick cottage and carried an ornate clock tower on its roof.

Inside, emphasis was on visibility. Cages were uncluttered and brightly lit, so the animals could be seen at all times. (Cement floors and tile walls also made it easy for zookeepers to clean cages.) Visitors were often allowed to view the animal at close range from all sides, an uncomfortable situation for a wild animal that needed a dark corner in which to hide when feeling threatened.

Life was even more uncomfortable for animals in smaller zoos and traveling menageries. Sketches of Polito's Royal Menagerie in the Strand, London, show a variety of animals in cages the size of packing crates. Monkeys crouch above the heads of a bored lion and tiger who have little room to turn around, much less walk. A few steps away, a lone elephant peers through the bars of its cage with a defeated air.

Lack of light and ventilation made these smaller zoos decidedly unpleasant, especially on warm days. The gloomy, smelly environment offended many visitors, who chose not to return after a first look.

This dissatisfaction with zoos went hand in hand with a growing concern for the welfare of animals. Around 1820, the British House of Commons passed a law that forbade cruelty to large domestic animals such as horses and cattle. Societies for the Prevention of Cruelty to Animals were organized shortly thereafter. In the United States, the Humane Society was founded in 1877 as a protector of both children and

The Small Mammal House at the National Zoo shows the stark, cramped quarters in which many zoo animals lived earlier in this century.

Different species of animals that would normally not live in the same environment were often forced together in menageries.

animals. The Audubon Society took up the cause of protecting wild birds and animals just before the turn of the century.

Most of this concern was directed at farm animals and pets. At least one man, however, dreamed of making zoos more pleasant for both animals and visitors. That man was Carl Hagenbeck.

New look in zoos

Little from Hagenbeck's early life would indicate how great his later contributions to zoos would be. Born in Germany in 1844, he ran a small zoo at the age of fifteen, then abandoned that to become an animal dealer and collector. In that role, Hagenbeck was responsible for acquiring thousands of animals for zoos and circuses. He was also responsible for thousands of animal deaths.

Collecting animals at that time was often a cruel and wasteful practice. Hagenbeck once pointed out that young elephants and rhinos "cannot as a rule be secured without first killing the old ones." The same practice applied to a variety of animals. Hagenbeck and other collectors learned that it was easy to capture a young monkey after shooting its mother because the baby stayed close to its mother's body after it had fallen out of the tree.

No one kept track of how many animals died as a result of these collecting expeditions. Death rates were high as the animals endured the strain of being captured, transported over rugged ground, and then shipped across the ocean. One expedition, not involving Hagenbeck, recorded the loss of seventy-six out of eighty-four animals caused by unfavorable conditions on the voyage home.

By the time Hagenbeck reached middle age, he was the most famous European animal dealer of his time. He was also ready to use his talents and reputation for another purpose. He writes:

> Now at last I am in a position to carry out my long-nursed project of founding a zoological park of a totally different kind from anything that had been before attempted. I desired, above all things, to give the animals the maximum of liberty. I wished to exhibit them not as captives, confined to narrow spaces, and looked at between bars, but as free to wander from place to place with as large limits as possible, and with no bars to obstruct the view and serve as a reminder of captivity.

Using the money he had saved while collecting animals, Hagenbeck began work on his dream. He bought land on the outskirts of Hamburg, Germany, and hired hundreds of workers. With steam

Carl Hagenbeck, the most famous animal collector of all time, acquired thousands of animals for zoos and circuses.

Hagenbeck's animal-collecting expeditions caused thousands of animal deaths. An 1893 cartoon proclaims "Hagenbeck Is Coming!" and shows fearful animals fleeing for their lives.

shovels, spades, and wheelbarrows, they moved tons of earth, built "mountains," and dug moats at Hagenbeck's direction.

The Carl Hagenbeck Tierpark opened in 1907. From the beginning, visitors were spellbound by what they saw. Gazelles, antelopes, and zebras seemed to move in total freedom across grassy meadows. A pride of lions basked in the sun almost directly behind them. Visitors could not see the enormous invisible moats Hagenbeck had created to separate the animal groups and ensure their safety.

The zoo was an engineering marvel. Virtually all cages and bars had been removed. Pens were open-air wherever possible. Sunshine, water, and grass replaced the dark, dirty surroundings that visitors had tolerated before. Animals were grouped by habitat and lived much as they would in the wild.

The idea of exhibiting exotic animals in replicas of their natural environments delighted the public. Eventually other zoos began to copy Hagenbeck's design, even though the process of creating landscape exhibits was very expensive. By 1913, London's Regent's Park Zoo had constructed the Mappin Terraces, rocky mountains for its wild sheep and goats. In 1919, the St. Louis Zoological Gardens (St. Louis Zoo) adapted Hagenbeck's style for its bear dens.

A need for arks

With time, effort, and imagination, dedicated people had begun to transform the look of zoos. Still, few recognized the uniqueness of the animals they cared for. Few noticed that wild animal populations were shrinking. Few realized the need for improved facilities, for research, and for educating the public.

Many years passed before zoo philosophy underwent a change. Not until after the mid-1900s did anyone begin to see zoos as arks, safe places for animals that had been victims of humankind's ignorance and abuse for too long.

2
A New Breed of Zoo

IN SPITE OF Carl Hagenbeck's influence on their physical appearance, zoos of the early 1900s were hard on the animals. Some enclosures were open-air; the rest were boxlike, barred, and generally uncomfortable. Animals were neglected or mistreated, often because of the ignorance or carelessness of their human caretakers. Monkeys huddled outdoors in freezing weather. Zebras hobbled across their pens on overgrown hoofs. Giraffes broke legs walking on slippery concrete. Keepers made some effort to keep their charges healthy, but everyone knew that dead animals could be replaced from the wild.

By the 1970s, animal lovers, including thoughtful zookeepers, had begun to notice shortcomings in zoo conditions and were demanding that they be corrected. As Palmer Krantz, director of the Riverbanks Zoo in Columbia, South Carolina, observes:

> You could see a shift in the public's attitude toward zoos. Wildlife shows on television were a big influence. They showed you animals running free in the wild, their behavior, the importance of ecosystems. . . . The Disney company and other theme park operators had an effect, showing how

(Opposite page) Recognition of the wretched conditions in some zoos gave birth to a new breed of zoo. Baringo giraffes have lots of room to roam in this spacious enclosure at the Bronx Zoo. The sign tells all about living habits of the giraffes.

stimulating exhibits could be and, by comparison, how old-fashioned were those in many zoos.

The definition of a "good" zoo was no longer one with the biggest animals or the best elephant or pony rides. Rather, good zoos were considered those that had begun to give the best care to the animals themselves. Many elements of animal welfare needed attention as zoo officials began working to ensure the comfort and well-being of their charges.

Personal space

One of the most important elements of animal comfort was a roomy enclosure. Even the best zoos could not provide the miles of territory that

Many zoo animals today can move and interact freely in large enclosures. But even these areas cannot offer the miles of territory found in the wild.

animals such as gazelles, zebras, and elands (ox-like African antelope) once enjoyed in the wild. Still, responsible zoo directors worked to supply enough space to allow animals to move and interact freely. Birds were placed in spacious aviaries where they could fly for short distances. Monkeys, if not given trees and vines, were supplied with an abundance of ropes and pipes over which to climb.

Comfort for most zoo animals also meant that their flight distance—the distance they allowed an enemy to approach before they tried to escape—was observed. This distance varied for each animal, depending on its size. Heine Hediger, behavior specialist and one-time director of the Zoologischer Garten (Zurich Zoo) in Switzerland, explains:

> As a rule small species of animals have a short escape distance, large animals a long one. The wall lizard can be approached to within a couple of yards before it takes to flight, but a crocodile makes off at fifty. The sparrow hops about unconcerned almost under our feet, thus like the mouse, having a very short flight distance, while crows and eagles, deer and chamois for instance, have much longer ones.

Disaster could occur if flight distances were violated. Panicky animals injured themselves trying to escape. Aggressive animals such as bears attacked when a visitor unwisely stuck an arm inside a cage.

Careful zookeepers began keeping visitors back from the animals through the use of guardrails or moats. They also provided a place at the back of the enclosure for the animal to rest or hide from constant public exposure.

Natural habitats

A significant contribution to zoo animals' comfort was the growing popularity of habitat

In the Lied Jungle exhibit at the Henry Doorly Zoo, visitors can catch a glimpse of the plants and animals that would occupy a real tropical rain forest.

exhibits similar to those created by Hagenbeck. This kind of exhibit might range from sand and cacti in the burrowing owl enclosure to a multitude of plants and animals in the Lied Jungle, a miniature rain forest found at the Henry Doorly Zoo in Omaha, Nebraska.

Early attempts to create habitat exhibits sometimes resulted in disaster. When the San Diego Zoo first set up a forest for its Malayan sun bears, the animals "shredded the trees, rolled up the sod, plugged the moat—and then one attempted a fast break over the wall. Spectators went scrambling . . ." reported *Time* magazine. Other exhibits had their own unique problems.

With time and experience, adjustments were made and displays were successfully completed. Today, the largest and most complex displays seem to allow visitors to step into the wild when they view them. Lied Jungle covers one and one-half acres and includes 2,000 species of exotic plants and 130 species of animals. Parrots, monkeys, and giant fruit bats share space with pygmy hippos and Malayan tapirs. The African Savanna exhibit in Seattle, Washington's Woodland Park Zoo is an open plain on which zebras, giraffes, and gazelles graze next to monkeys, hippos, and several species of birds. In the African Rock Kopje (pronounced "copy") exhibit at the San Diego Zoo, artificial volcanic lava rocks provide a home for badgerlike rock hyraxes, plated rock lizards, klipspringers (small antelopes), and pancake tortoises.

Habitat exhibits not only let visitors form a more authentic picture of animals and their natural behavior, they allow animals to live under conditions similar to those normally found in the wild. Penguin Encounter at Sea World in Orlando, Florida, maintains near-freezing temperatures and produces six thousand pounds of

In the African Savanna exhibit at Washington's Woodland Park Zoo, zebras share space on an open plain with several species of animals, including giraffes, monkeys, and hippos.

Visitors observe endangered wolves in a natural setting at the Arizona-Sonora Museum.

"snow" (finely ground ice) each day for the Antarctic birds. Woodland Park's Tropical/Nocturnal House in Seattle and Cleveland Zoo's Creatures of the Night exhibit in Ohio display nocturnal animals such as bats, anteaters, and porcupines in a realistic twilight world that shows them at their active best. At night, brighter lights are switched on to simulate daylight so the animals can sleep.

Some zoos have taken a different approach to the problem of creature comfort. They emphasize species that are native to the region of the zoo. For example, the Arizona-Sonora Museum in Tucson, Arizona, houses desert cats, bats, and rattlesnakes. The Taronga Zoo in Sydney, Australia, emphasizes animals like the duck-billed platypus, the koala, and Leadbeater's opossum.

Behavioral enrichment

In their efforts to provide comfort to the animals, zoo experts learned that they could not ignore the problems of boredom and psychological stress. When animals are confined alone or in cramped quarters, boredom is common and easy to spot. A big cat paces endlessly to and fro in its cage. A motionless gorilla stares into space. A rhino walks a never-ending circle in its tiny yard.

Concerned with these behaviors, Zurich's Heine Hediger was one of the first to begin studying the psychological needs of zoo animals. His findings, published in the mid-1950s, influenced the thinking of many modern animal experts.

Hediger discovered that, although space was important to animals, a large cage by itself was not enough to meet their needs. A monkey, for instance, was bored if it lived alone. The addition

A gorilla in an old, indoor enclosure exhibits the boredom common among animals confined alone or in cramped quarters.

of trees, ropes, and a few more monkeys improved its behavior enormously.

"In reality, the quality of the space at the disposal of the animal is of the greatest importance for its welfare," Hediger writes.

The experiences of other early zookeepers supported Hediger's findings. Animals seemed to enjoy having something to do. In the early 1900s, orangutans and chimpanzees at the Bronx Zoo charmed visitors by playing "tea party," just like human children do, sitting at small tables and eating out of dishes. Zoos that owned sea lions discovered that the animals quickly learned swimming and balancing tricks and displayed them for the crowds with little prompting.

Zoos discovered that sea lions quickly learned swimming and balancing tricks and liked to perform for crowds.

As time passed, however, most zoos stopped encouraging such anthropomorphic behavior (imposing human characteristics and behavior on animals). Instead, they tried to enhance natural activity that would normally occur in the wild. Los Angeles Zoo behavior specialist Thaya du Bois explains:

> There has been a dramatic shift in attitude—a coming to realize that animals may be better off when they have some control over how they spend their time. This is difficult because there seems to be a natural inclination in people to do things for animals—to cut fruit into pieces or peel a hard-boiled egg. This helps feed the animals, but does not take care of their behavioral needs, the need to do for themselves.

Many changes were simple yet effective. Bears, given a large plastic bucket, sometimes used it as a ball, and sometimes filled it with water to pour over their heads on a hot day.

Du Bois notes that at the Los Angeles Zoo:

> We . . . drill holes in logs and stuff the holes with raisins, seeds, and other tidbits. Our lemurs and monkeys have to pick the food out with their fingers. . . . We hide tiny dabs of food in the nooks and crannies of rocks—cooked rice, peanut butter, anything that gets the animals moving around and foraging.

Animals outsmart keepers

At times, the animals outsmarted their keepers by catching on too quickly to the new proceedings. Keepers at the Minnesota Zoological Gardens (Minnesota Zoo) decided that the sloth bear, a small, slow-moving creature who spent his days sleeping, needed more exercise. To stimulate his interest, they smeared honey and insects into the cracks of a log in the exhibit.

The idea worked, but the animal proved to be a faster learner (and a faster mover) than anyone expected. "The bear can glom up all the honey

When keepers at the Minnesota Zoo tried to make slow-moving sloth bears work harder for their meal of insects and honey, the bears surprised their keepers by catching on quickly.

you can smear into the crevices and all the crickets and mealworms you can put out in ten or twenty minutes and be back sleeping in the tunnel," admits curator Jim Pichner.

Importance of diet

A balanced diet was another factor necessary for creature comfort. In most well-managed zoos, signs near the exhibits reminded visitors that junk food snacks such as peanuts and cotton candy would lead to sick or overweight animals. At the same time, caretakers regularly consulted nutritionists and veterinarians to ensure that each animal received the diet it needed to remain healthy.

Given the number of animals involved, enormous amounts of food were required. Every year at the National Zoo in Washington, D.C., more than two thousand animals consumed thousands of pounds of meat, potatoes, vegetables, and fruit, plus tons of hay and grain. In addition, almost every species had its special preferences. Thousands of mice and rats (painlessly killed and frozen) were provided for the small carnivores, birds of prey, and reptiles. Fresh bamboo kept the pandas healthy.

Balancing diets was no easy task. Giving a slab of meat to a carnivore provided only some of the nutrients it would get in the wild by eating the entire body of its prey, including stomach, liver, and bones. Vitamins and minerals needed to be added. Elephants were fed oats and corn, plus a variety of fruits and vegetables to round out their diet of hay.

Zoo experts soon learned that improper diet could affect animals in unexpected ways. This was demonstrated in the late 1970s with golden lion tamarins.

When captive populations of these squirrel-sized golden-orange monkeys reached alarmingly

Boxes of food are unloaded at the San Diego Zoo for consumption by the zoo's many animal species. Veterinarians and nutritionists help to ensure that each animal eats the foods it needs to remain healthy.

National Zoo researchers successfully increased the reproductive rate of golden lion tamarins by adding protein to their diet.

low levels, researchers faced the fact that the animals were at serious risk of becoming extinct. Almost 98 percent of their rain forest habitat in Brazil had been harvested, and a survey suggested that fewer than 250 animals survived in the wild. To make matters worse, the few tamarins in captivity had problems producing young.

Researchers at the National Zoo tackled the problem, determined to find a solution. As a part of their studies, they concentrated on the tamarins' food preferences. The findings were significant. While captive tamarins had always been fed a basic diet of fruit, researchers discovered that, in the wild, they ate protein as well. After adding cottage cheese, eggs, and protein-rich insects to their diet, reproduction improved. The zoo population of tamarins began to increase.

Social requirements

Correcting the tamarins' diet solved only part of the problem. Researchers discovered another factor that affected reproduction—family relationships. Tamarins were social creatures, preferring to live in families made up of a pair of adults plus offspring of different ages. Female adults, however, were fiercely territorial.

In zoos, young females were routinely removed from the group and placed in a separate cage fairly early in life to avoid attack from the dominant or ruling female. Unfortunately, these younger females later made terrible mothers. They ignored and sometimes killed their offspring.

After studying wild tamarin behavior, researchers saw the reason for this problem. In the wild, young tamarins learned parenting skills from the older couple in the group. With the early separation that occurred in zoos, they could not. The zoo began leaving young females with the family for a slightly longer time. The females then learned necessary skills and thereafter successfully raised their own young.

Over time, zoo experts recognized that, like the tamarins, most species have social and behavioral requirements that need to be met for safety, reproductive success, and emotional well-being. Requirements differed from species to species. For instance, researchers learned that older addra gazelles attack young animals if they are not separated from the herd before they are six months old. Baboons do not react in this manner, but live peacefully together in large groups. Gibbons (a type of ape) choose a "traditional" family setting of two parents plus young if given the chance.

Sometimes the needs of one species are the opposite of another. Wolves prefer a clean den and need an outside location to deposit waste. The slow loris (a large-eyed relation of the monkey) considers a clean cage a hardship. "Every time its cage is cleaned out this animal has to drink

In addition to proper diet, it is important that zoos meet the different social and behavioral requirements of each species. The slow loris, for example, prefers a dirty cage to a clean one.

As the zoo's primary caretakers, keepers clean cages, feed the animals, and maintain records of behavior.

incredible quantities of water straight away and sprinkle the nice clean floor systematically just like a watering-cart," Hediger reports.

Who meets the needs?

With endless animal needs to be satisfied, running a modern zoo is no one-person task. Dozens of workers manage a variety of demands and responsibilities that range from taking tickets to doctoring a sick elephant.

At the head of every zoo is a director who oversees all activities and suggests changes or improvements that will benefit the zoo. The director is also involved in fund-raising and other public relations projects. Although the position has traditionally been filled by men, there are now more than a dozen female zoo directors in the United States.

Numbers of zoo employees work in public services, operating snack bars and gift shops, selling tickets, and maintaining the grounds. Others work as keepers, curators, and veterinarians, providing services vital to the comfort and health of the animals.

Keepers are the primary caretakers in any zoo. They clean cages, feed the animals, and maintain records of behavior. They know the likes and dislikes of their charges. Skilled keepers are usually the first to recognize an illness or injury in their animals.

"I feel an important part of my job is to take care of them mentally, as well as physically," explains one keeper of the great apes at the National Zoo. "If they want to play, I put down whatever I'm doing and indulge them."

Curators deal with species and help set policy for the zoo. They oversee keepers, help create exhibits, and choose information for signs and displays. They work to make a trip to the zoo a positive experience for every visitor. As one curator explains:

> We want the public to feel that they have seen something beautiful, that they have been informed, that they liked what they saw, that they want to come back again and bring their friends to share this experience.

Working behind the scenes of any good zoo are the veterinarians, men and women who fight disease and treat injuries. Their jobs are seldom simple. Exotic species become ill easily, and their symptoms are often hard to detect. Some diseases, once introduced, could easily wipe out an entire exhibit of rare animals. Veterinarians must closely check any new animals that come into the zoo, making sure that none carry disease, pests, or parasites.

Dr. Richard Montali proved a veterinarian's worth in 1976, when trouble struck the National Zoo. After two unexpected animal deaths, Montali diagnosed the problem as yersiniosis, a type of

A veterinarian at New Orleans' Audubon Zoo gives a gorilla his annual physical. Veterinarians work behind the scenes to fight disease and treat injuries.

tuberculosis contagious to both animals and humans. Watchful for other cases, the doctor was ready when three more animals died shortly thereafter.

Again the cause of the deaths was yersiniosis. Working quickly, Montali directed that all animals and people at risk be given antibiotics. He quarantined the affected area of the zoo, insisted that keepers wash their hands before eating, and set up a program to get rid of the suspected carriers—wild rodents and pigeons. Thanks to prompt action on everyone's part, the disease was quickly contained with no further deaths.

Working closely with veterinarians are scientists and technicians who research the little-known details of exotic animal anatomy and behavior. Their findings are also important to zoos. For instance, information about reproductive cycles of many species has added to the success of captive breeding programs in many zoos.

Room for improvement

Of the hundreds of well-run zoos that exist worldwide, no two are exactly alike. Some are modest, edged by city streets. Others sprawl boldly across the countryside.

All share certain qualities, however. The grounds are clean, the atmosphere cheerful and informative. Animals are in good condition, physically and mentally. They produce young (a sign of comfort), although breeding is controlled. Experienced caretakers are available to observe the animals' habits and preferences and to teach visitors about the animals and their importance in the wild.

The new breed of zoo is more animal-friendly than those of the past. Zoo supporters cannot relax, however. Even the finest facilities have their failings. And the continued existence of inadequate, ill-managed zoos is a painful reminder that there is still much room for improvement.

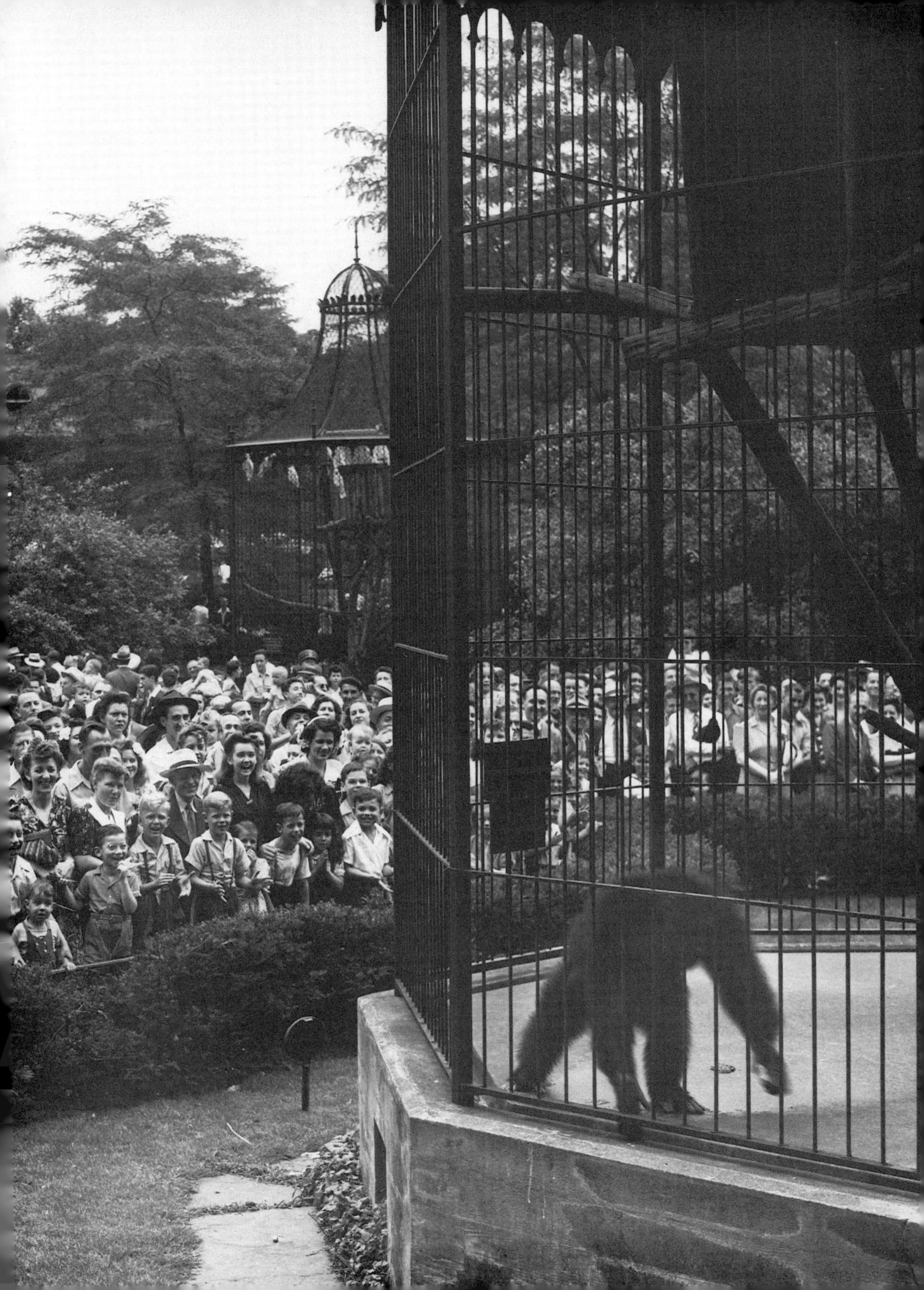

3

Problem Zoos

KEEPING PACE with the changing times, modern zoos have transformed themselves with extraordinary speed. Airy habitat exhibits allow animals to live in greater comfort. Creative educational programs remind the public of its responsibility to wildlife and the environment.

"Our professionally run zoos and aquariums of the 1990s are a world apart from the cement-and-bar-caged menageries of earlier in this century," says Jack Hanna, director emeritus of the Columbus Zoological Gardens (Columbus Zoo) in Ohio.

Yet not every zoo is professionally run. Statistics show that, for every responsible institution such as the San Diego or National Zoo, there is at least one that fails to meet accepted standards.

Many of these zoos are of the traveling or roadside variety, often dirty and rundown. Others, like Slater Park, have more subtle shortcomings. Cages are small and boring. Exhibits are considered postage stamp collections—one or two of as many kinds of animals as possible. Signs or programs that educate the public are nonexistent. Animals give birth to litters of young, and no thought is given to the overcrowding that results.

In his book *The Crowded Ark*, environmentalist Jon Luoma expresses a reaction that is common to many who view animals in such a setting: "I

(Opposite page) The typical 1940s zoo exhibit was often not designed for the animal's well-being. Many modern zoos strive for a more natural setting, but problem zoos still exist today.

could see no justification for such places, where animals ripped from natural environments are put on display for human gawkers, their social and psychological needs ignored."

Zoo scandals

While the public is quick to recognize and criticize small, inferior zoos, they are sometimes slow to notice the shortcomings of larger institutions. Keeping a watchful eye on the conditions of established zoos is essential. Although most zoos are respected and admired today, they are not always free of mistakes, mismanagement, or even scandal.

In 1984, conditions at the Grant Park Zoo (now Zoo Atlanta) in Georgia shocked those who discovered them. Animals were living in filthy, cramped cages. Zoo personnel had apparently

Grant Park Zoo's Kodiak bear pit. Two of the zoo's Kodiak bears died while on loan to a roadside menagerie.

failed to provide balanced diets for the animals. Some animals were overweight, others starving. Two Kodiak bears had been loaned to a roadside menagerie whose manager killed them because of "unruly behavior." Twinkles the elephant, a favorite at the zoo, died after being sold to a small traveling circus that transported her around the country in the back of a pickup truck.

Prospect Park Zoo in Brooklyn, now a member of the NYZS/Wildlife Conservation Society, also came under criticism in the late 1980s for its heavily barred cages, old-fashioned animal houses, and smelly seal pool. The zoo gained notoriety after several animal tragedies occurred there. In one incident that highlighted poor zoo security, police shot two polar bears after the animals attacked and killed a teen who had sneaked unnoticed into their enclosure.

Because of the negative publicity, Grant Park Zoo and Prospect Park Zoo made changes in policies and exhibits. They are now on the way to becoming two of the finest zoos in the world. Another famed institution, Regent's Park Zoo in London, is not.

Problems at Regent's Park Zoo

Regent's Park, for years the model of a first-class modern zoo, came under attack in the early 1990s. Having suffered from a shortage of funds for decades, the zoo had not been able to upgrade its exhibits. Little attention had been given to conservation or to visitor education. According to one former staff member, the zoo had "poor maintenance, mediocre exhibits, lackluster programs, disregard for good visitor services, bad management, and especially an adherence to an outmoded philosophy."

Even zoo enthusiasts realized that something was wrong when officials announced in 1991 that

A bored gorilla stares through a wire cage at London's Regent's Park Zoo, once a model of a modern first-class zoo.

the zoo would close. The British government, which had previously provided grants, was unhelpful this time. "My view is that people in the 1990s believe that confining animals in a 37-acre site like Regent's Park Zoo is not appropriate. There will be no more government money for Regent's Park," stated the minister of environment.

In spite of the zoo's uncertain future, a $1.85 million donation from the emir of Kuwait allowed the ailing zoo to remain open through 1993. Many of its animals were sent to Whipsnade Wildlife Park, a nearby facility that is also a part of the London Zoological Society.

Traveling and roadside zoos

Although zoos like Regent's Park still satisfy an undemanding portion of the public, traveling and roadside zoos offend almost everyone. Experts estimate that there are as many as one thousand of these menageries in the United States. Some place that figure higher, at around fifteen hundred.

An article describing this type of zoo appeared in 1992 in *The Animals' Agenda*, an animal rights magazine. The article profiled a tiny Louisiana roadside menagerie, colorfully titled the Snake Farm. One example of the farm's exhibits was a scrawny, ex-circus chimpanzee named Joe. Joe did nothing but sit in his small, empty cement cell all day. The door to his cage was rusted shut, a reminder of the twenty years of solitary confinement he had endured.

A variety of menageries and animal exhibits fall into the category of traveling or roadside zoos. One type is the traditional elephant ride concession that often follows a carnival from town to town. Another is the single exotic animal used to lure tourists into gift shops or shopping centers.

Ivan, a lone gorilla in Tacoma, Washington, is one such exhibit. Ivan has lived alone in the back of a store since 1964, in spite of complaints from animal activists that a cement room is no place for a wild animal. Finally bankruptcy proceedings against the store's owner in 1993 produced results that the protests did not. A plan was approved to relocate Ivan to a more natural habitat: the new gorilla colony at Zoo Atlanta in Georgia.

The 1993 movie Free Willy *focused public attention on poorly run marine parks. Its star, Keiko the orca whale, lives in a cramped tank in a Mexico City amusement park. Keiko suffers from poor health and receives inadequate medical care.*

Bored and abused

The lives of Joe and Ivan demonstrate the inadequate, sometimes abusive, conditions that many zoo animals endure every day. Mistreatment may stem from ignorance, but many owners and managers simply care only for the money they bring in. The abuse is not limited to the United States. Reports from Europe, Asia, and South America cite similar conditions there.

A relatively well-known instance involves Keiko, the orca whale who helped call attention to inadequate marine parks in the 1993 movie

Animals that have little social interaction and physical activity often show their stress by displaying a lack of energy.

Free Willy. With filming completed, Keiko spends his days in a cramped tank at an amusement park in Mexico City. According to Jim McBain, director of veterinary medicine for the Sea World parks, the water in the tank is at the wrong temperature and has poor quality. Keiko is still growing and suffers from a worsening skin condition. The park lacks money to improve conditions for the animal and hopes to sell him.

Animals forced to live in poorly run zoos commonly are stressed or bored by inactivity and too little social interaction. As environmentalist Marcia King writes in *The Animals' Agenda*:

> Running animals can't run, burrowing animals can't dig, flying animals can't fly. . . . Social animals have no companions, pack animals no herd, shy animals no privacy. Prey animals live side by side with their predators.

Symptoms of stress are easy for animal psychologists to recognize: lack of energy, swaying or rocking, endless pacing, even self-mutilation, when animals bite or chew themselves or pull out their fur. Some animals become unexpectedly aggressive, lashing out if given the chance. Chimpanzees, for instance, rush to the front of their enclosures to shake the wire walls, scream, and spit at visitors.

In badly run zoos, diets may be irregular and unbalanced, with no thought given to the animals' weights or nutritional needs. Meals are supplemented by leftovers from visitors' picnic baskets. Sometimes a zoo will sell peanuts or other tidbits for visitors to toss into the cages. In one Florida zoo, animals reportedly spent their weekends eating nothing but day-old baked goods, purchased cheaply from a nearby bakery. Many animals were sick by Monday morning.

Inferior zoos also neglect other elements that contribute to the well-being of animals. Cage floors are covered with urine, feces, and vomit. Animals often are infested with parasites or infected with disease. Unskilled workers fail to notice early symptoms of illness. Many times, finding a veterinarian willing to treat exotic animals is difficult.

"Most of the time [second-rate zoos] hire whoever they can get. They don't have the money to hire a zoologist or to have a staff vet there for the animals," says Laura Bevan of the Humane Society of the United States, one of the nation's oldest organizations for animal welfare and protection.

Unnecessary deaths

Some animals are physically abused by owners who lose patience with them. Some are injured or killed as a result of poor security. At roadside and traveling zoos, fences may be inadequate, even nonexistent, leaving the animals unprotected from mischief-makers.

Even at the best zoos, vandalism has been a recurring problem. Incidents have occurred worldwide. The Moscow Zoo reported one case in which a family of kangaroos was stabbed to

Children feed geese during a visit to New York's Joyland miniature zoo in 1953. For many families, the Sunday afternoon drive to the local zoo has been replaced by television, video games, and other forms of entertainment.

death. Five deer were beaten in New York's Central Park Zoo. Philadelphia teens stoned several flamingos at the zoo there.

"It is doubtful whether any American zoo has escaped vandalism in some form by sadistic, ignorant, or dimwitted humans," points out Peter Batten, former director of the San Jose Zoological Gardens. But while well-managed zoos make every effort to protect their animals, poorly run zoos often have no money for or interest in doing so.

Discounting violence, animals die every year as a result of unhealthy conditions that exist at poorly managed zoos. Some die because of overcrowding, a condition that also causes cannibalism of young and increased anxiety and illness in adults.

Former San Diego Zoo keeper Lisa Landres reports that deaths are especially common in traveling zoos, where "the animals are kept in small cramped transport cages. . . . There have been instances where animals have died from lack of ventilation and extreme heat. They've also been abandoned in the trucks."

Who is responsible?

With growing public concern for animals and the environment, many people wonder how problem zoos continue to exist. The answer is that many do not. Significant numbers of traveling and roadside zoos in the United States have shut down in recent years. Some closed because of public outrage. Some closed for lack of business. Television and video games have replaced the traditional Sunday afternoon drive when families would stop at a roadside zoo or entertainment park.

The American Zoo and Aquarium Association (AZA), formerly known as the American Association of Zoological Parks and Aquariums, has some influence over zoos. AZA had its beginnings in the early 1920s under Dr. Harry Wegeforth, founder of the San Diego Zoo. Today, the organization strives for professionalism and communication within the zoo community. It encourages policies such as humane and responsible treatment of animals, captive breeding programs, and educational programs for visitors. It also promotes zoo legislation in Washington, D.C. In the United States, almost 160 zoos are members of AZA.

Although AZA sets the standards for high-quality zoos, its powers of enforcement are limited. Membership is denied zoos that ignore animal welfare and public education. AZA member zoos can be censured or removed from membership for failing to comply with the organization's directives. For instance, the Columbus Zoo in Ohio temporarily lost its AZA membership in 1992, after zoo officials borrowed a pair of giant pandas from China for the city's

A national zoo organization criticized the Columbus Zoo for borrowing a pair of giant pandas from China for a city celebration. The organization viewed the celebration as a poor reason to subject the endangered pandas to a long-distance trip.

celebration of Columbus's journey to America. The animals are highly endangered, and long-distance transfers can endanger their health. The Convention on International Trade in Endangered Species (CITES) discourages unnecessary traffic in these animals. The animals were not ill treated, but a city celebration was viewed as a poor reason to subject them to a potentially dangerous journey.

Although AZA has only limited control over zoo conditions, other regulations for animal exhibitors do exist. In the United States, the 1971 Federal Animal Welfare Act acknowledged public concern for captive animals and set some minimum standards for their maintenance: cage size, sanitation, and so forth.

Several U.S. agencies are in charge of enforcing these and other, more general, animal welfare regulations. The Department of Health and Human Services looks for animal diseases that can threaten humans. The Department of the Interior watches over endangered species still living in their natural environment. The Department of Agriculture (USDA) is concerned with the conditions of both domestic and wild animals, including their health, living conditions, and diseases that can be passed between them.

In spite of this variety of agencies and regulations, unqualified persons continue to buy, sell, and exhibit animals. Permits to set up zoos in the United States are relatively cheap and easy to get. The USDA, with primary responsibility over roadside and traveling zoos, often has too few inspectors and too few funds to check out all violators.

Despite the variety of agencies charged with the job of ensuring the welfare of captive animals, many still live in inadequate enclosures.

After twenty-seven years of living alone indoors, Willy B. enjoys comfort and companionship in his newly remodeled gorilla exhibit at Zoo Atlanta.

"The regulations used by the USDA to enforce the Animal Welfare Act are vague, meaningless, and worthless," Lisa Landres charges. For instance, no actual sizes are listed for enclosures. Owners can get away with providing a small cage for a lion, even though it would be healthier in a much larger one.

Most USDA inspectors are sincere in their concern for animals. Still, many are not trained to recognize zoo shortcomings. Inspectors also find it difficult to track down violators who travel from place to place. Visitors often complain first to a local animal protection organization. By the time the USDA is notified, the menagerie has disappeared, and sometimes has even changed its name.

Hope for the animals

Further government action—tougher requirements and stricter penalties—could help make substandard zoos a thing of the past. Changes that have been demanded by animal welfare groups, however, are sometimes blocked by zoo and circus lobbyists. They fear that some restrictions will adversely affect even those who treat animals in a responsible and caring way.

In the meantime, some cities and states have begun to do what they can to discourage inferior, abusive menageries, especially traveling zoos. New York, California, Florida, and others have laws that regulate trade and transport of animals within each state. In Florida, state officials have taken responsibility for inspecting roadside and traveling zoos, forcing them to upgrade or close down. Toronto and several other Canadian cities banned exotic animal acts, including those featured in circuses and traveling zoos. Although the ban in Toronto was later lifted, some tough regulations remain.

With a growing awareness of the needs of animals, communities today are more likely to complain about the presence of irresponsible, ill-managed zoos. Concerned citizens do not hesitate to demand that the animals be rescued and placed in improved surroundings.

Some animals that are rescued have not been permanently harmed. Willy B., a gorilla who lived alone for twenty-seven years at the former Grant Park Zoo in Atlanta, now enjoys green grass and female companionship in the remodeled gorilla exhibit there. For others, however, help comes too late. Joe the chimpanzee, eventually rescued from the Snake Farm and placed in an animal sanctuary in Texas, never recovered his health. He died of heart failure shortly after his arrival.

Joe's death makes a tragic point. The day of badly run zoos is passing, yet the ones that remain take a terrible toll on the animals. Those who value these creatures agree that the end of abusive menageries cannot come quickly enough. As Michael Mackintosh, manager of Stanley Park Zoological Gardens in Vancouver, British Columbia, says, "We can't just keep these animals to entertain us [anymore]. Those days are over."

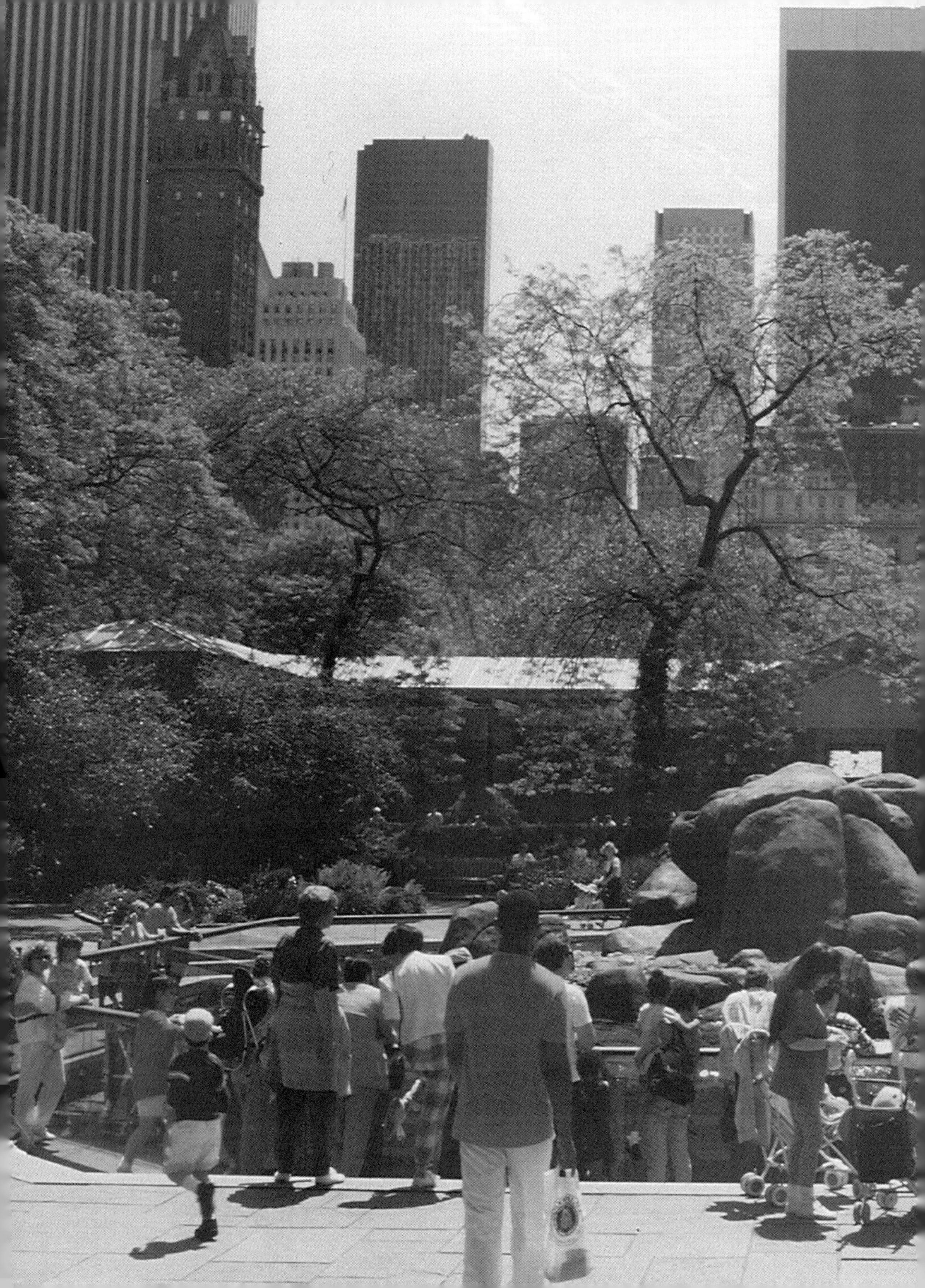

4
Do We Have the Right?

ALTHOUGH ZOOS have worked hard over the past two decades to update their exhibits, their services, and their philosophy, those who visit zoos are not always satisfied with what they experience. New habitat exhibits contrast sharply with old enclosures that have not yet been remodeled. Even in the newest exhibits, evidence of civilization is everywhere. Some trees and greenery are made of concrete and plastic. Climates are thermostatically controlled. Feedings are scheduled. Animals are confined within artificial boundaries.

The public has come to recognize that zoos, no matter how much they improve, can only imitate nature. This recognition has given rise to several troubling philosophical questions. Some have begun to question the rationale for confining animals. They ask themselves if people have the right to take animals from the wild and place them in zoos, even under the best conditions.

On the other hand, many believe that humankind has not only a right but a duty to support zoos. Animals face great dangers in the wild. Many species are becoming extinct. If zoos are in a position to help save animals, they have

(Opposite page) Skyscrapers behind Central Park Zoo serve as a reminder that no matter how much zoos improve, they can only imitate nature.

a responsibility to do so even when that means keeping the animals in captivity.

But devotion to the goal of saving endangered species has led to a different problem: overcrowding. Successful breeding programs result every year in thousands of surplus zoo animals. These animals must be sold, traded away, or killed because there is no room for them in zoos and because returning them to the wild is often much more difficult than it sounds. Many people question whether zoos should have this power of life and death over their charges.

These questions—whether humans have the right to cage animals, to keep them in zoos for their own safety and survival, and to control every aspect of their lives—are not easily answered. They are nevertheless worthy of consideration by all who have an interest in animals and the unique relationship humankind has forged with them.

Out of the wild

Until the mid-1900s, the right of people to collect animals for zoos went almost unquestioned. Collecting expeditions provided animals for new exhibits and replaced those that regularly died in captivity.

The king of the collectors was Carl Hagenbeck, creator of the first zoo without bars. Another famous collector, Frank Buck, thrilled the public in the 1930s with his jungle exploits detailed in his book *Bring 'Em Back Alive*. Buck was a colorful character and returned to the United States with the first anoa (a wild ox), proboscis monkey, and siamang (a type of monkey) ever seen in American zoos. Unfortunately, the title of Buck's book was misleading. A great many of the animals he imported died before they arrived.

Many of the animals captured by collector Frank Buck never made it to America alive.

Early zoo directors were collectors as well. William M. Mann, head of the National Zoo from 1925 to 1956, personally led collecting expeditions to Africa, Cuba, and elsewhere. In 1926, he returned with more than thirteen hundred animals, including a pair of giraffes, the first to be exhibited at the National Zoo.

Over time, however, collecting practices came under criticism. Zoo managers, dealers, and environmentalists began to realize that they were threatening the future of wildlife when they killed dozens of animals in order to capture others. Laws were passed in countries around the world to limit the collecting.

During the Convention on International Trade in Endangered Species (CITES) in 1973, more than fifty nations agreed to restrict the buying, selling, and transport of endangered species. Passage of the 1973 Endangered Species Act

Nations worldwide have agreed to restrict and monitor collection, sales, and transport of endangered species. A baby Asian elephant arrives at the Lincoln Park Zoo in 1960. Feeding instructions appear on the outside of the transport crate.

A captive-bred Siberian tiger cub is weighed in at the Minnesota Zoo. Today, more than 80 percent of mammals living in zoos are captive-bred.

effectively banned the hunting, collecting, and threatening of rare wildlife in the United States.

These regulations did much to eliminate the zoo practice of taking rare animals out of the wild. And, because of their success in breeding exotic animals, American Zoo and Aquarium Association (AZA) zoos today can say that most of their exhibits are captive-bred, born in captivity. More than 80 percent of mammals living in zoos are captive-bred. Almost 75 percent of new birds in captivity are born in zoos. The numbers are almost as high for reptiles.

In spite of that, irresponsible, poorly managed zoos and traveling menageries still purchase animals that have been taken illegally from the wild. Great numbers of parrots and other exotic birds, as well as langurs (long-tailed monkeys), tapirs, chimpanzees, orangutans, and gorillas, die each year while being smuggled across borders.

Speciesism

Zoo policies of breeding their own animals for exhibits are more humane than methods used in the past. Yet, the question remains whether wild animals should be held captive at all, especially for human pleasure and education.

A number of people believe that confining wild animals in zoos is cruel and unnecessary. They believe that animals can best be cared for in the wild, where they belong. "There is no need for zoos," states Amy Bertsch of People for the Ethical Treatment of Animals (PETA), a group that aims to investigate and abolish animal abuse in the United States. "We don't believe animals should be kept in captivity for any reason. Zoos teach people that it is acceptable."

People like Amy Bertsch believe that zoos are guilty of speciesism when they place animals in captivity. Speciesism is defined as discrimination or prejudice based on species, especially human

Protesters carry signs objecting to the capture and confinement of three dolphins at a Chicago aquarium. Some people believe that confining wild animals in zoos and aquariums is cruel and unnecessary.

discrimination against animals. Simply put, speciesism is the belief that humans are better than other species. Humans who do something to an animal that they would not do to a person are, according to this line of reasoning, guilty of speciesism.

"There really is no rational reason for saying a human being has special rights," says Ingrid Newkirk, PETA's cofounder. "When it comes to feelings like pain, hunger and thirst, a rat is a pig is a dog is a boy."

Playing God

Those who believe in speciesism feel that it allows zoos to act as if certain species are more important to our world than others. For instance,

Some zoo critics charge that when zoos work to save an endangered species like the Bengal tiger (pictured) and ignore other endangered animals, they are practicing speciesism—discrimination based on species.

zoos work to save endangered giant pandas and Bengal tigers, but ignore animals such as the California gnatcatcher, a small gray bird also nearing extinction.

Some people question the right of zoos to "play God" when they set aside time, money, and space to save certain species and not others. According to the laws of nature, surviving species are those most able to adjust to changes in the environment. Those that cannot adjust become extinct. Zoos, however, disrupt that natural process by trying to save the very animals that are in the most danger.

Zoos respond by pointing out that much of the danger to animals has been caused by human activities. People have destroyed natural habitats. People have killed millions of animals for sport or profit. People should also take responsibility for repairing or halting some of the damage they have done. They can do this in zoos.

"We're not playing God, we're simply trying to save some of these things while we can. Once they are gone, they are lost forever," states animal specialist Johnny Arnett.

Protectors

At the same time that some people question the right of zoos to keep animals in captivity, others maintain that zoos serve a valuable purpose when they protect animals.

Says Toby Styles, executive director of support services at the Metro Toronto Zoo:

> People might argue that a certain animal might be better off in the wild, but it's no picnic out there. In one afternoon in Kenya I saw more dead wildebeests than there have ever been in the entire history of zoos.

The world has always been a dangerous place for animals. Today, the spread of civilization has pushed many species to the edge of extinction. Recognizing the danger, some people see zoos as uniquely able to save endangered species. They believe that zoos should make every effort to protect as many animals as possible.

Because animals are territorial creatures, used to living within limited regions in the wild, zoo boundaries are not as restricting as they might appear. In addition, life in the zoo has many real benefits. Animals live longer because they are safe from predators (including humans). While animals in nature suffer from parasites, wounds, or disease, animals in the zoo are watched over by experienced keepers and veterinarians who give them plenty of food and water and tend to their every physical need.

Thanks to the comfort and protection found in captivity, today more animals of some species live in zoos than in the wild. Several herds of Pére David's deer, creatures that look like a cross between a deer, a goat, a donkey, and a cow, exist in captivity, while only a small number have been

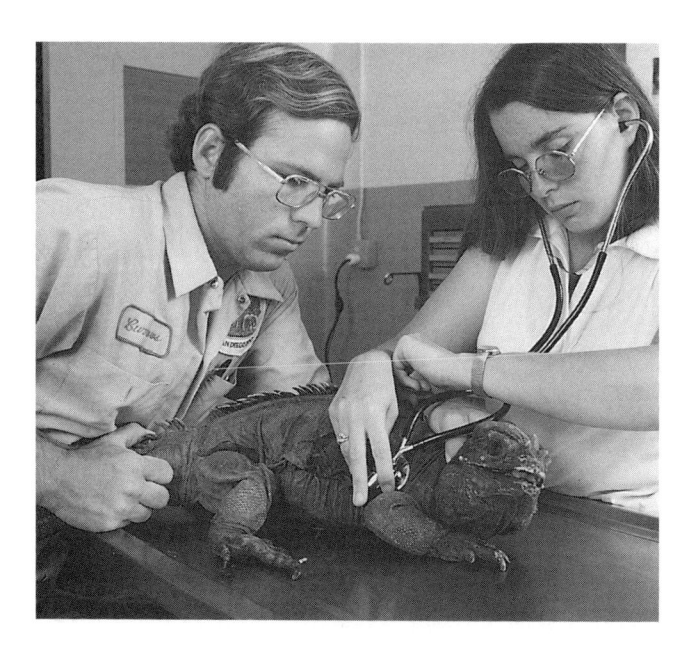

With caring and experienced keepers and veterinarians who tend to an animal's every need, zoos preserve many species that otherwise would die out in the wild.

introduced into their native China. Przewalski's horses, stocky, pony-sized animals, are believed to be extinct in Mongolia, where they originated. More than six hundred of these animals survive in zoos around the world.

Outside the walls

As protectors, zoos do more than just shelter animals within their walls. They support projects that preserve animals in their natural habitats as well. The Minnesota Zoo directs a portion of its income to the Ujung Kulon National Park in eastern Java. The park holds most of the world population of Javan rhinos. The NYZS/Wildlife Conservation Society helps protect loggerhead turtles off the coast of Georgia as just one of its more than 150 projects in forty-one nations throughout the world. The Jersey Wildlife Preservation Trust, a zoo and breeding center on the island of Jersey in the English Channel, sponsors research and conservation projects in Brazil, Mexico, Madagascar, and other countries.

Extinct in the wild, more than six hundred Przewalski's horses survive in zoos around the world.

Educating the public

Those who see zoos as protectors of endangered animals also believe that these institutions must teach the public about the need to conserve animals and their habitats. Although this education could take place using books, television, and videos, zoos provide an experience that pictures cannot. As William Conway of the NYZS/Wildlife Conservation Society says:

> At a zoo or conservation park . . . you confront the living, breathing animal. There is an immediacy of enormous value and importance. It's something that cannot be Xeroxed. The power of that confrontation—as concerns our feeling about wildlife and our struggle to preserve it—cannot be gainsaid, ever.

The design of the shark exhibit at Point Defiance Zoo in Washington allows visitors to discover the power and range of the sharks' sense of smell.

Modern, well-run zoos take their role as educators seriously. They grab visitors' attention with exhibits that include thought-provoking pictures and graphics. At the Point Defiance Zoo in Tacoma, Washington, visitors to the new shark exhibit discover the power and range of the big fishes' sense of smell as they are drawn through the exhibit with a series of questions. Inside the entrance of the Nocturnal House at Seattle's Woodland Park Zoo, colored visuals of animal eyes cover the wall and help explain the features that allow creatures to see in the dark.

Education at the zoo is more than just interesting information placed near the exhibits. Many zoos offer classes, particularly for children.

Some, like Zoo Atlanta, set aside certain months for certain animals—"Team Up for Tortoise Month" or "Apes Are Great Month"—and provide contests, slide shows, and storytelling hours. The Baltimore Children's Zoo has recreated key ecosystems found in the state of Maryland. They include a marsh aviary, an abandoned beaver lodge, and a farmyard for youngsters to study.

At the Columbus Zoo "children study everything," says spokesman Jack Hanna:

> They paint, they draw . . . they watch how rattlesnakes rattle and how sharks breathe. The lucky ones may witness a birth in the hoofstock yard or see how a keeper trims an elephant's toenails. Learning is fun at the zoo.

Dealing with the surplus

While a trip to the zoo can be both fun and educational, zoos have a darker side that visitors

Many zoos offer classes for children that make learning about animals fun.

never see and rarely hear about. Overcrowding and the need to get rid of surplus animals is a problem that almost every zoo must face. According to John Grandy of the Humane Society, "We estimate (that all zoos together) produce 8,400 animals a year in excess of any particular facility's needs, usually as a result of captive breeding."

AZA zoos generally follow certain guidelines when they have no room for an animal. The first is always to try to sell, loan, or give the animal away to a qualified institution, usually another AZA zoo. Since there are so many surplus animals, however, space in qualified facilities is limited. Then zoos can either give or sell the animal to a dealer who then resells it, or they can cull the animal—put it to death. These last two solutions, more than the others, raise troubling questions about the right of zoos to decide the fate of animals in their care.

Although zoos intend that surplus animals will be treated with care and respect after they leave the zoo, there are no guarantees that this will be the case. Once an animal has been sold to a

Exotic animals, including Siberian tigers, have been hunted on illegal game ranches.

dealer, zoos have little control over where it will eventually be placed.

Dealers often take zoo animals to wildlife auctions where they are sold to the highest bidder. Some animals go to individuals who pay high prices for exotic pets but know little about how to care for them. Other animals end up in research labs or in the movie and television industry. Some are purchased by game ranchers who sponsor illegal hunting expeditions.

Canned hunts

The Texoma Hunting Wilderness in southern Oklahoma was this type of ranch. It made the news in 1990 when state and federal wildlife agents investigated the 160-acre preserve. Investigators found animals, many thought to have been purchased from zoos and wildlife auctions, being held in pens too small to meet their needs. Owner Charles Bartholomew's records indicated that he had charged customers from $1,000 to $4,000 for the chance to hunt exotic animals, including African lions, North American buffalo, and grizzly bears.

The hunts themselves hardly deserved the name. Animals were corralled in a large field as hunters sat above, spraying them with .450-caliber bullets.

"Four-fifty, that's enough—more than enough—to kill an elephant," one game warden points out. "This is what we call a canned hunt. It's like opening a can of sardines and saying you went fishing."

The Texoma ranch was closed in 1990. Still, the statistics regarding other game ranches are troubling. More than four thousand game ranches—some devoted solely to birds—continue to operate in the United States alone. And, although AZA zoos are taking even greater care

Public outrage prevented the Minnesota Zoo from culling a surplus Siberian tiger. Zoos have received a great deal of criticism for culling, the practice of killing healthy animals to relieve overcrowding.

when they place surplus animals, many zoos do not belong to that organization. Those zoos sell surplus animals to anyone who wants them, with little thought for the suffering that may result.

Culling

If people question the right of zoos to sell surplus animals to dealers, they take an even stronger stance when it comes to culling, the practice of killing healthy animals to relieve overcrowding.

"The very idea of culling conflicts with what zoos are all about: the study, appreciation, and conservation of wild animals," stresses William Conway, longtime director of the NYZS/Wildlife Conservation Society.

The idea of zoos killing animals they have worked so hard to save is troubling. With the number of extinct species climbing every day, many people challenge any zoo's right to take an animal's life just because there is no room for it in captivity.

In *The Crowded Ark*, John Luoma recorded public reaction to a 1984 incident when Minnesota Zoo officials decided to cull a surplus Siberian tiger. Zoo personnel had already advertised the cat for sale, then offered to give it away to any zoo with proper facilities to care for it. When no one seemed to want the animal, officials reluctantly decided it should be culled.

Before that could happen, the story made the news. Reporters charged that endangered species were being "sentenced to death row" at the Minnesota Zoo. The public was outraged and wrote thousands of letters, insisting that the tiger be spared. Phone lines were tied up for days. In the end, the zoo bowed to public opinion and announced that it would spare the tiger. The animal was eventually placed in the Shanghai Zoo.

Other zoos have experienced similar reactions when they consider culling—or have actually culled—an animal. However, they point out that culling is beneficial for species even if it means sacrificing individuals. Animals that are too old or unnecessary for breeding are humanely killed to create space for animals that will produce strong, healthy offspring. Culling, while not popular, is therefore a practical option, given the limited space available in most zoos.

A humane alternative

Because the policy of selling or culling zoo animals is disturbing, many people wonder if zoos could perhaps find more humane ways to deal with the surplus animals in their care.

One obvious option is to release surplus animals into the wild. Not only would this solution

Many zoo animals would not survive if released into the wild. For instance, polar bears that have lived in zoos do not know how to hunt and have no body fat. They would quickly freeze or starve to death if returned to the Arctic.

ease the problem of overcrowding in zoos, it would help rebuild dwindling animal populations in nature.

The suggestion has one serious flaw, however. The majority of zoo animals have never lived outside of zoos. Most have never learned skills such as hunting for food, avoiding predators, or surviving through a long winter. Studies have shown that, if animals are not prepared from birth, they will be almost helpless on their own in the wild.

As animal dealer Ken Chisholm points out in response to a suggestion that polar bears be returned to the Arctic, "[The bears] don't know how to hunt, they don't have any fat—they're going to freeze or starve to death before you fly home."

Debate over the relationship between humans and animals and the place of zoos in that relationship is not likely to be settled in the near future. Some say zoos are exploiting animals when they deprive them of their freedom in the name of conservation and education. Cathryn Hilker of the Cincinnati Zoo disagrees. She says:

> I don't think we're exploiting animals, I think we're using animals. There's a difference between using something honestly and exploiting something for your own ends. . . . The honest truth is that these animals are disappearing. . . . The honest truth is that if we don't do something about it, it's going to happen. I believe that these animals cause awareness. I believe this is a . . . good use of these precious creatures.

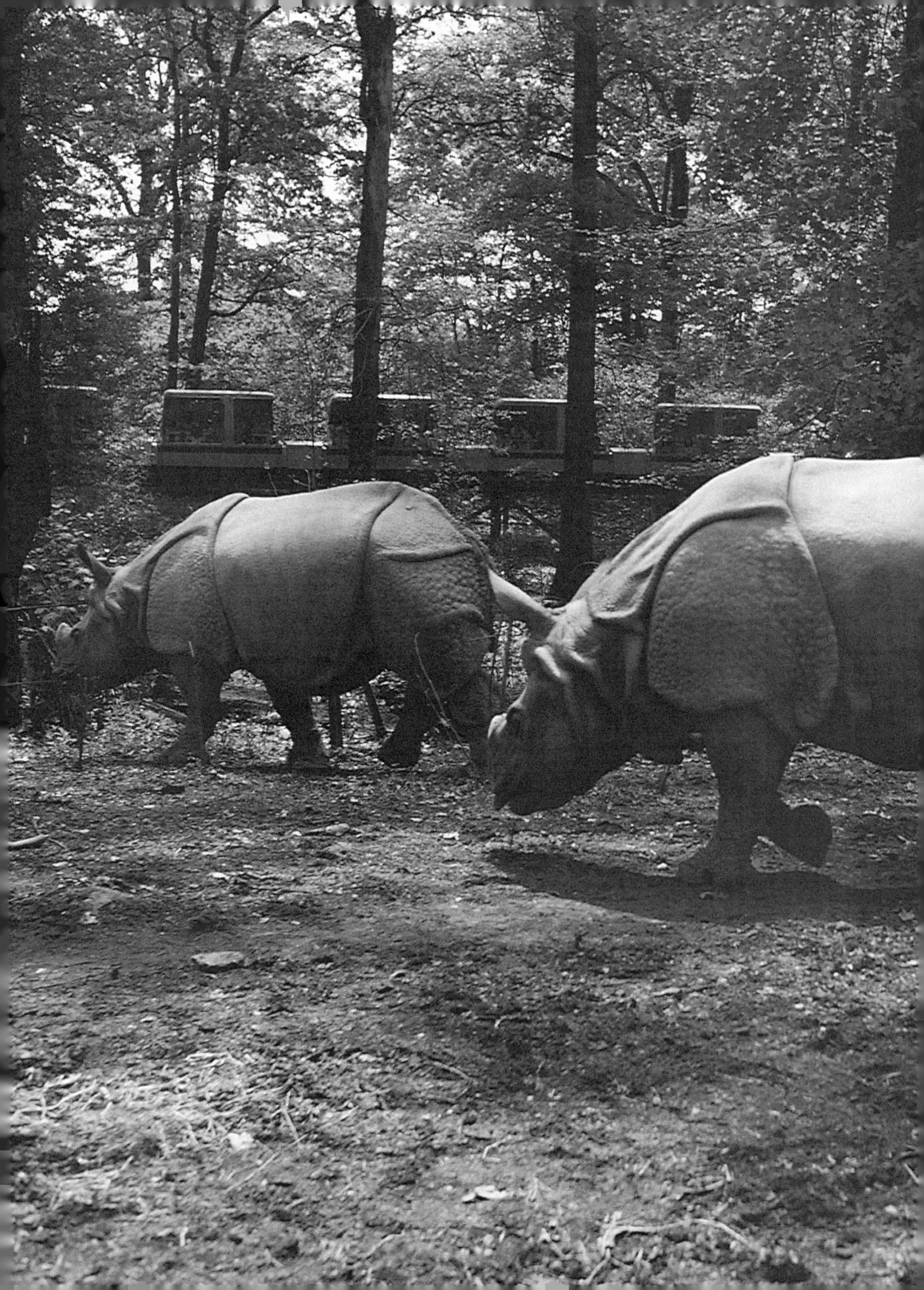

5

Zoos as Arks

EVERY DAY, a little more wilderness disappears from our world. Human populations continue to grow. People disrupt forests, jungles, and other wild areas as they spread over the earth, clearing land, planting crops, and changing the environment. With these changes, they leave thousands of species without habitats.

"Species have become highly adapted to their habitat, like keys that fit precisely in ecological keyholes. Without the keyholes, the keys cannot function," says Jon Luoma.

When species cease to function, they become extinct. Faced with the rising number of extinctions, zoos have chosen to help curb the losses. Today, saving endangered species has become one of the top priorities of modern zoos throughout the world.

Epidemic extinctions

The fact that animal species vanish from the face of the earth is neither strange nor unexpected. Historically, extinction has been the norm for all living things. Scientists estimate that more than 90 percent of all species that ever lived are now extinct.

The increasing speed at which the disappearances are taking place is unusual, however. In

(Opposite page) A tram ride provides Bronx Zoo visitors a glimpse of the endangered rhinoceros. As modern day arks, zoos have made saving endangered species a top priority.

As a result of hunting and farming practices, the passenger pigeon became extinct in North America in the early 1900s.

earlier times, extinction was a slow process. Dinosaurs, for example, vanished at a rate of about one species every thousand years.

As time passed, the extinction rate accelerated. Between 1650 and 1850, animals and birds such as Stellar's sea cow (a seal-like creature), the dodo and the great auk (flightless birds) became extinct after sailors and hunters killed thousands for food. In the early 1900s, passenger pigeons, once so numerous in North America that they blocked the sun when they migrated, disappeared as a result of hunting and loss of their forest habitat to farming.

One of the latest, and most dramatic, losses was that of the Javan tiger. Knowing that the animals were highly endangered, zoo experts in the 1980s had pushed to get a breeding group into captivity. Conservationists disagreed, arguing that the animal should be left in the wild and protected there. A decision was put off.

Then "one day the question was asked, 'How many Javan tigers do we have left?' The answer was none—they were extinct, gone," relates William Conway.

Today, a great percentage of extinctions, like that of the Javan tiger, take place in tropical regions around the world. Complex evergreen rain forests cover less than 6 percent of the earth's surface but are home to an estimated 50 to 90 percent of plant and animal species.

Important as rain forests are as natural habitats, they are rapidly disappearing. More than two-thirds of the rain forests in Asia and South America have been logged, burned, paved, or converted to pasture. Millions of acres of forest are being

A section of rain forest smolders after being burned by farmers. Deforestation threatens countless species of animals.

destroyed every year. Some scientists estimate that at least five hundred plant and animal species, many of them insects, disappear annually. If that rate continues, a fifth of all remaining species may be lost in the near future.

Help for endangered species

Researchers have understood for some time that plants and animals, including humans, depend on one another for life and that losses of species threaten the balance of nature. These losses also risk much of the beauty and variety of life. "It suddenly and powerfully became clear that many of the living creatures we all held so dear simply would not exist much longer," says William Conway of the NYZS/Wildlife Conservation Society.

The International Union for the Conservation of Nature and Natural Resources (IUCN), a branch of the United Nations, was established in 1948 with the purpose of supporting conservation efforts worldwide. It regularly published the *Red Data Book*, a record of endangered and threatened animals. In 1961, the IUCN set up the World Wildlife Fund, the world's largest private conservation organization. Groups such as the Nature Conservancy, the Sierra Club, and Greenpeace also did their best to call attention to wildlife and related issues.

Yet the losses continued. In the United States, the Endangered Species Act of 1973, designed to protect endangered plants and animals, was only partially effective because of its lack of funds. In other parts of the world, protection of wildlife was imperfect as well. Farmers in India and Africa herded their cattle within the boundaries of national parks, overgrazing native vegetation and invading territory set aside for Asian lions and African elephants. Disasters such as drought and war in Africa and other continents took their toll on humans and animals alike.

Focusing the collections

With captive populations of endangered species already on hand, zoos began to see themselves as arks, places that could protect animals that were in danger of becoming extinct. However, because space was limited, zoos had to decide which species they could support most effectively.

Traditional zoo animals, known as charismatic megavertebrates—animals such as elephants, rhinos, lions, and zebras, whose presence traditionally drew the most visitors—were well represented. Lesser-known mammal species, such as tree kangaroos or lemurs, were seen less often, as were most species of insects, reptiles, birds, amphibians, and fish.

Zoo personnel began taking steps to correct this problem. They decided to focus on endangered

The National Zoo traded away or sold primates to make room for the reddish-brown lesser pandas.

species that reproduced easily in captivity. To do this, they eliminated some exhibits that could be seen in other zoos, added other exhibits, and enlarged populations to make up breeding groups. The National Zoo, for example, traded away or sold half of its primate collection (especially chimpanzees) to make room for lesser pandas and marmosets (rare South American monkeys). The Philadelphia Zoological Gardens expanded their bird collection to include a Hummingbird House. The Cincinnati Zoo invested more than one million dollars in an Insect World exhibit.

Inbreeding

As zoo experts focused their collections and entered the battle to save endangered species, they were dismayed to learn that inbreeding threatened to undo all their efforts. Inbreeding occurs when generation after generation of closely related animals produce young. After many gen-

Inbred white tigers are often born swaybacked and cross-eyed. Such problems with inbreeding have resulted in changes in zoo breeding practices.

erations, inbred members of a species possess genes (hereditary material) from only a few animals. Thus, all inbred animals have very little genetic diversity; they are all very similar.

As diversity is lost, inbred populations are often less able to adjust to changes that may occur in their environment. For instance, if an inbred herd no longer includes at least a few animals that can survive with very little water, the entire population will die during a drought.

Harmful traits that might not often appear in larger populations become serious hazards with inbred ones. Individuals often suffer from disease and physical abnormalities. For example, many inbred white tigers, popular exhibits at the Cincinnati Zoo and others, are swaybacked and cross-eyed. Cheetahs, all of which are highly inbred, have weak immune systems. In addition, they have difficulty becoming pregnant and producing healthy young.

For years, inbreeding had been a common state of affairs at zoos. Zoo experts were aware that it could cause problems with reproduction, but for the most part, they ignored the fact. Then, a 1979 study at the National Zoo revealed statistics too chilling to be ignored. Inbred animals there were bearing fewer and fewer healthy offspring. Findings concerning the scimitar-horned oryx, a type of antelope, were most dramatic. Only slightly more than 5 percent of non-inbred young oryx died in the first six months of life, but *all* inbred offspring died in that same period.

Zoo experts realized that they needed to act quickly to correct the problem, or losses due to inbreeding would soon spell disaster.

Species Survival Plans

By 1981, AZA zoos had begun to respond to the inbreeding threat by creating Species Survival

Plans (SSPs). The plans changed the way zoos bred their animals. They also changed the way zoos worked together.

Species Survival Plans ensured that the widest possible range of genes were passed from generation to generation by mixing and matching unrelated animals for breeding. Participating zoos recorded vital statistics such as an animal's parents, ancestors, place of birth, age, and sex into a computerized database. The most well known is the International Species Information System (ISIS), a program created by conservation biology specialist Ulysses S. Seal. Zoos on six continents and in fifty-five countries throughout the world participate in the system, which is based at the Minnesota Zoo.

Computer programs made evaluating and matching animals relatively easy. Plans might read, "Breed 975 F(female) with 1023 M(male) in the year 1998," or "760 M has behavioral problems and is not recommended for breeding."

Vanilla, a lowland gorilla at Hermann Park Zoo in Houston, refused to mate with her would-be suitor, sent on a "breeding loan" from a Colorado zoo.

ZOO SUCCESSES WITH ENDANGERED SPECIES

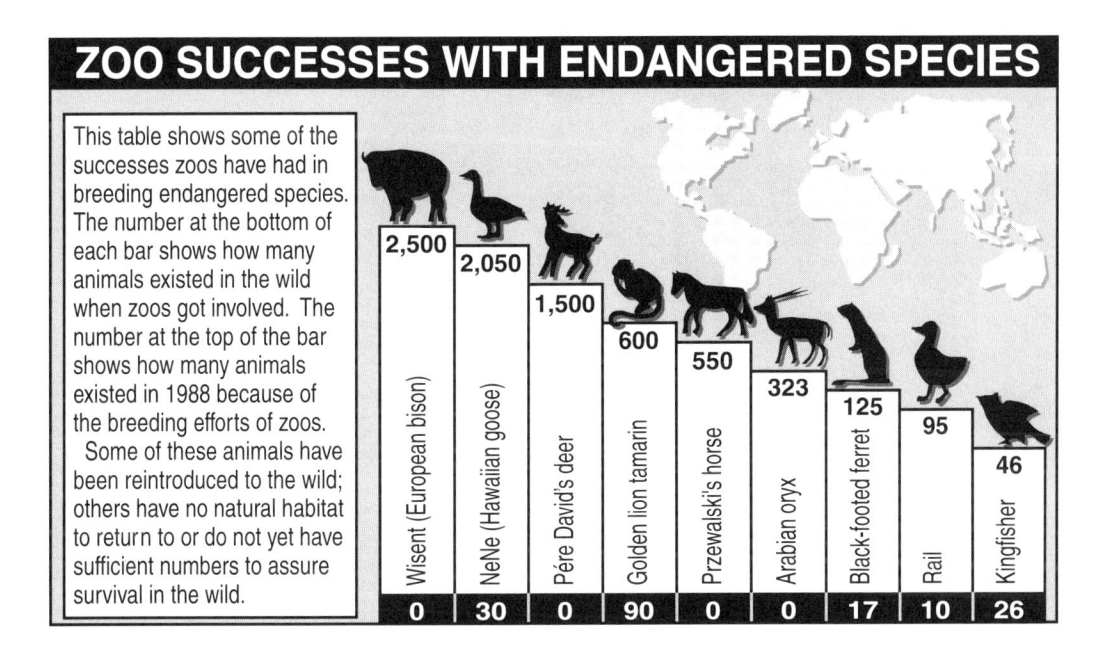

This table shows some of the successes zoos have had in breeding endangered species. The number at the bottom of each bar shows how many animals existed in the wild when zoos got involved. The number at the top of the bar shows how many animals existed in 1988 because of the breeding efforts of zoos.

Some of these animals have been reintroduced to the wild; others have no natural habitat to return to or do not yet have sufficient numbers to assure survival in the wild.

Species	1988	Wild when zoos got involved
Wisent (European bison)	2,500	0
NeNe (Hawaiian goose)	2,050	30
Pére David's deer	1,500	0
Golden lion tamarin	600	90
Przewalski's horse	550	0
Arabian oryx	323	0
Black-footed ferret	125	17
Rail	95	10
Kingfisher	46	26

After a match was made, experts shipped one of the animals to the other at a participating zoo. These "breeding loans" did away with much of the competition that once existed between facilities. Instead of trying to outdo each other, zoos now worked together to achieve a common goal, that of securing the future of endangered species.

Although SSPs have proven to be valuable tools for saving animals, certain problems have arisen that need to be addressed. There are more than one thousand different endangered species, yet fewer than one hundred are represented worldwide in supervised breeding programs. Zoos hope to increase the number to two hundred by the year 2000, but the need for plans to aid the remainder is critical.

In some cases, despite the best efforts, SSPs cannot prevent inbreeding of some species because there are so few surviving members of those species. Sometimes animals produce young that do not meet the needs of the SSP. For instance, the zoo may need a male tiger, but a female is born. Natural occurrences such as these hamper the plans and add to the number of surplus animals.

So do hybrids, a mix of two or more species, born in the days before breeding was carefully supervised. White tigers are hybrids, as are one-third of all orangutans found in U.S. zoos. Because zoos prefer to breed purebred animals, hybrids are generally not acceptable for SSPs.

In addition to these practical complications, the whole idea of managed breeding offends some. "Many people think [it's] unnatural," says Michael Soule, founder of the Society for Conservation Biology. "But from that point of view the world has been unnatural since man first started to hunt and burn the savannas."

Conservation centers

Today, responsible zoo personnel take their role as conservationists seriously. Their goal is to slow the flood of extinctions until, as some demographic experts predict, human populations stop growing. At that time, problems such as global warming may be better understood. People might have started to rebuild the habitats they once destroyed, recreating homes for endangered species.

When that happens, zoos aim to be ready with as complete a collection of animals as possible. Species Survival Plans are vital to the success of that aim. So are conservation centers, fenced areas of countryside where endangered animals live almost as if they were in the wild, cared for by staff who ensure their well-being.

There are at least two advantages to conservation centers. First, animals are placed farther from people. Thus, they are more relaxed than they might be in a traditional zoo. Second, the centers' vast open spaces allow for larger groups of animals than would be found in an ordinary zoo. For instance, in the 2,100-acre San Diego Wild Animal Park, partner of the 100-acre San Diego Zoo, the herd of addaxes (large North African antelope) numbers at least sixty. The park also supports a herd of thirty slender-horned gazelles.

"That would be unthinkable in the typical [zoo] collection," points out one park curator. "They would have three or four at the most."

Several zoo-supported conservation centers exist in the United States. Besides the San Diego park, the Columbus, Cincinnati, Cleveland, and Toledo zoos have had a part in the creation of the Wilds, a 9,150-acre facility in southern Ohio. The New York Zoological Society's Rare Animal Survival Center is located on St. Catherines Island off the coast of Georgia. The National Zoo's 3,150-acre Conservation and Research Center is set in the Virginia countryside. The latter two

Animals at the San Diego Wild Animal Park enjoy a more spacious and relaxed setting than they would have in a more traditional zoo. Animals are more likely to produce offspring in this type of setting.

Whipsnade Wildlife Park in Great Britain is so spacious that just one of its fenced pastures could hold the entire 37-acre London Zoo.

facilities are off limits to the public, leaving the staff free to focus entirely on the animals.

Conservation centers also operate in other countries. Canada has the 220-acre Devonian Wildlife Conservation Centre near Calgary, and Great Britain has Whipsnade Wildlife Park, a 500-acre center. Known for its spacious, open-air enclosures, Whipsnade has at least one fenced pasture large enough to hold the entire 37-acre London Zoo.

Breeding and birth control

Zoo experts have learned that when hard-to-breed animals are placed in conservation centers, they are more likely to produce offspring. But experts also discovered that they needed to understand the mating habits of each species if they were going to breed some endangered animals successfully. Surprisingly, these habits vary widely.

In studying the habits of cheetahs, for instance, researchers learned that the big cats would not breed if they were forced to live in the same cage for any length of time. Indian rhinoceroses, on the other hand, needed plenty of time together before starting a family. And while most zookeepers knew that lions were not shy about mating in public, it took some time to discover that sable antelope seemed to prefer privacy for their romantic moments.

Over time, zoo experts have become highly creative when it comes to mating hard-to-breed animals. Because every species has its own schedule for reproductive cycles, some animals are monitored surgically to determine when they are most ready to mate. Efforts are then made to avoid disturbing them during that time.

Other species need different kinds of treatment. At the Cincinnati Zoo, experts administer hormones to Puerto Rican crested toads to stimulate breeding. At the National Zoo's Conservation Center, keepers remove and incubate the eggs from the nests of Florida sandhill cranes. The female will then lay a second pair of eggs about two weeks later, effectively doubling the number of young she produces. At New York's Rare Animal Survival Center, researchers learned that the maleo, an Indonesian bird, lays a single egg beside a geothermal vent (a crack in the earth's crust from which steam is released) in the wild. In the late 1980s, the first maleo chick outside of Indonesia was hatched after workers reproduced these nesting conditions at the center.

With the growing importance of controlled breeding, zoo experts often want to prevent births. At such times, they turn to birth control. Keepers give female animals birth control pills in

Zoo experts work diligently to ensure mating and reproductive success of hard-to-breed animals. Sometimes, such success requires that workers remove eggs from their nests and incubate them in carefully monitored laboratory settings.

A chimpanzee at Jerusalem's Biblical Zoo is fitted with an IUD to prevent pregnancy. Zoos often turn to birth control to prevent unwanted births.

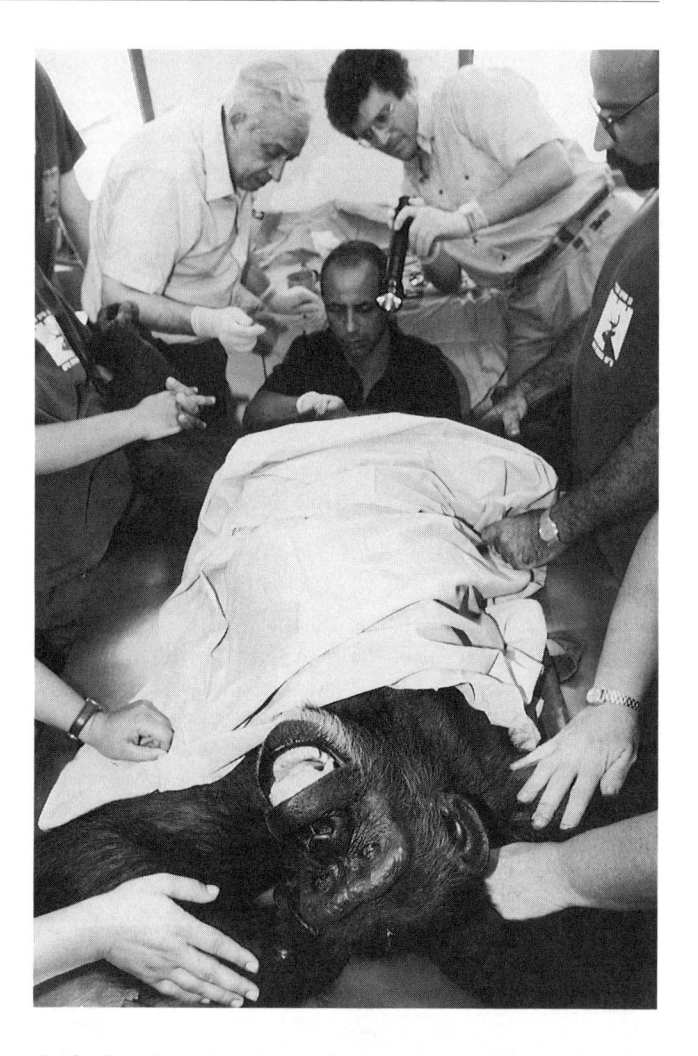

their food or implant slow-acting pills under the skin. The effects are entirely reversible so the animals can reproduce at a later time. When an animal is no longer wanted for breeding, more permanent contraceptive methods may be used.

Reintroduction

As populations of some endangered species became well established in zoos, managers began a long dreamed of project—preparing certain animals for reintroduction, or release, to natural habitats.

Even at the beginning, no one thought the process would be easy. While many people were delighted to think of zoo animals going back to the wild, others scoffed, claiming that the creatures had become too dependent on people to survive on their own. In many cases, civilization itself could cause problems. For instance, western ranchers were likely to shoot wolves that attacked their cattle, no matter how important the animals were to the zoo.

Zoo experts ignored the scoffing and made their plans. They knew that animals intended for release needed to be as wild as possible, so keepers carefully avoided contact with them. They also worked hard to teach behavior that would normally be almost instinctive outside of captivity. Live food was placed inside enclosures so meat eaters could practice stalking their prey. Animal models designed to look and move like predators were used to simulate attacks on smaller animals so they could learn to run and hide.

Success in the wild

The careful preparations paid off when reintroduction finally took place. In 1964, the last few wild Arabian oryx, a creamy white antelope with three-foot-long horns, had been rounded up and taken to the San Diego and Phoenix zoos. Their population in those zoos had grown to more than one hundred. In the early 1980s, a small herd of captive-born Arabian oryx was set free on the Arabian Peninsula. Under the protection of the sultan of Oman, the tiny herd survived. Today, herds of oryx again live in the wild in Oman, Jordan, Saudi Arabia, and Israel.

In 1984, workers released a group of golden lion tamarins, born at the National Zoo, into the Poco das Antes rain forest reserve in Brazil. Once the animals adjusted to their new home, they

Careful preparation by the National Zoo contributed to the success of the zoo's 1984 release of golden lion tamarins into the Poco das Antes rain forest in Brazil.

flourished. By 1991, females had produced more than fifty offspring.

In 1987, a pair of red wolves was released into the Alligator River National Wildlife Refuge in North Carolina. After being declared extinct in the wild in 1980, captive red wolf populations had grown, thanks to breeding programs in several U.S. zoos. By 1992, numbers of red wolves in the wild had climbed to twenty-seven, and four more animals had been released into Great Smoky Mountain National Park in North Carolina and Tennessee.

While small populations of black-footed ferrets and Puerto Rican crested toads were also successfully reintroduced to native habitats in the late 1980s and early 1990s, the reintroduction of the California condor in 1992 proved a more disappointing experiment. In preparing for the release, keepers at the San Diego Wild Animal Park kept young condors isolated from the public to avoid imprinting, a condition in which very young birds, if exposed to humans, may accept them as role models or "mothers." These imprinted young would then reject others of their own species, and would be helpless in the wild.

Two captive birds were released in January 1992, into the Sespe Condor Sanctuary in the Los Padres National Forest, northwest of Los Angeles. Hopes were high, but negative predictions proved correct. One of the birds died within the first year, a victim of pollutants found in a recreational lake near its new habitat. With only one member of the species left in the wild, breeding was impossible unless additional birds were reintroduced.

In spite of setbacks and failures, zoos remain dedicated to the goal of saving endangered species. Some people challenge their efforts, saying that they are doing too little, too late, and at too great an expense. These critics doubt that zoos will be able to save more than a fraction of species that are or will soon be in danger of extinction. They question if zoos will be able to raise the millions of dollars they will need to fund future conservation efforts.

It will take time for the doubts and questions to be answered. Meanwhile, zoo personnel will continue to educate the public and cooperate with others who believe that wildlife must be saved. In the words of William Conway, "Of course it's not enough. *Of course* it's not preserving the diversity of life on earth. But at least we're making a stab at it."

A California condor chick accepts food from a hand puppet designed to look like the bird's mother. Despite such efforts, the 1992 release of two captive birds into the wild was a disappointment.

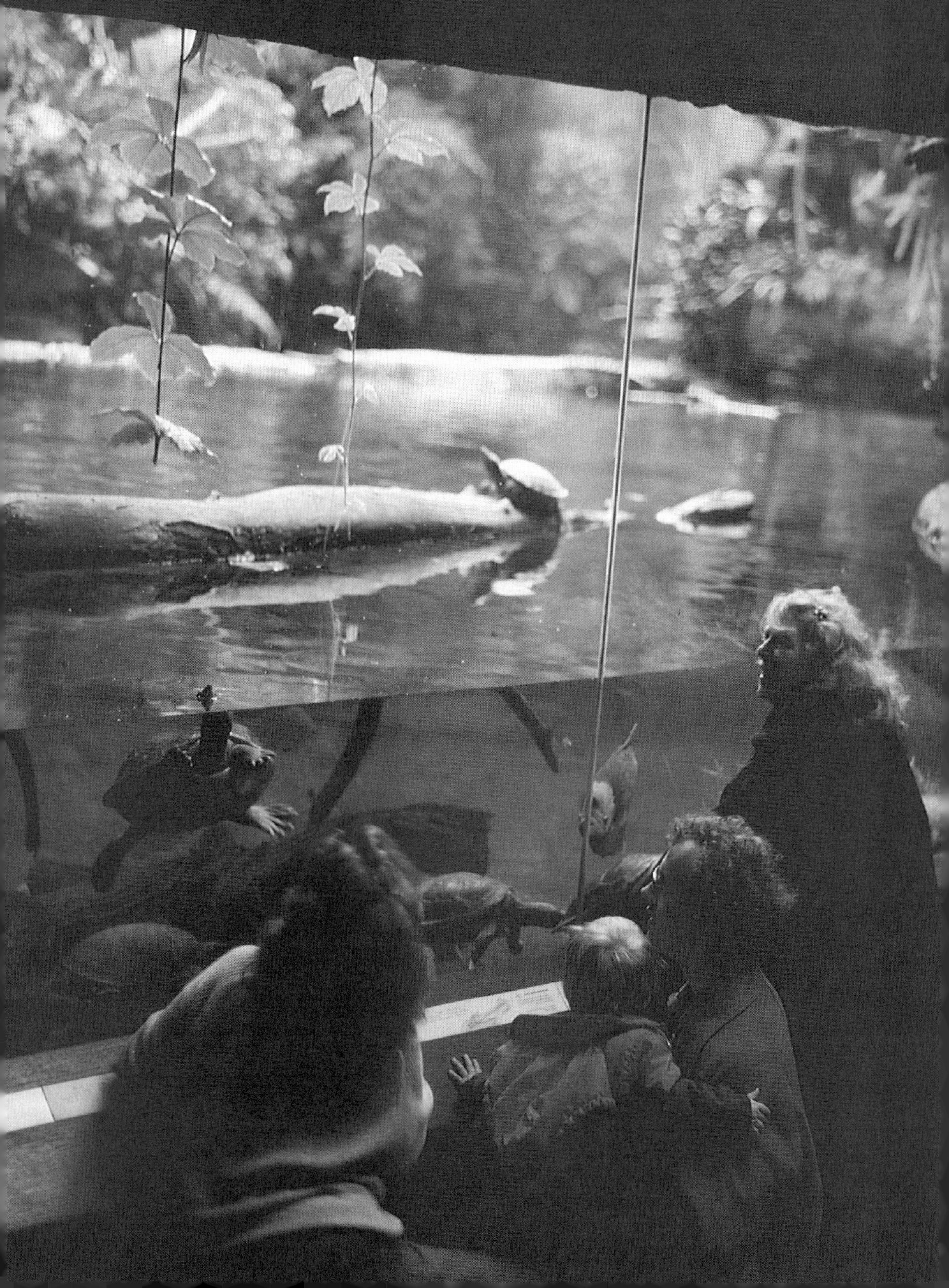

6
Zoos for Tomorrow

As ZOOS BECOME leaders in the effort to save wildlife, their future depends to a great extent on their commitment to the animals themselves. Zoologist and author George Schaller points out, "Zoos have no validity nowadays, no purpose, except to help protect and raise endangered animals and to raise public consciousness about the plight of wildlife."

By holding to that purpose, zoos have the potential to make valuable contributions to the environment. If not, they may have to make way for other, more effective, alternatives.

The Belize Zoo

Sharon Matola, of the Belize Zoo, is firmly committed to animals. Her success in spreading an environmental message to the people of that tiny Central American country has earned her much admiration.

A native of Baltimore, Maryland, and an enthusiastic scientist, Matola loves adventure. At the age of twenty, she became a trainee at the U.S. Air Force's jungle survival training school in Panama. After leaving the military, she performed as an exotic dancer and lion tamer in

(Opposite page) Survival for zoos of the future may depend on a commitment to protecting endangered animals and to raising public awareness about the plight of wildlife.

Sharon Matola's commitment to animals in the tiny Central American country of Belize has earned her a great deal of admiration.

Mexico. She then found work in Belize helping with an underwater fish survey. After completing the survey, Matola stayed in Belize to help handle native animals in a movie being filmed there.

When filming was finished, Matola discovered that the crew had gone, but the animals had been left behind. "Most of [the animals] had always lived in captivity and would never make it in the wild," she explains. "In good conscience I couldn't release them."

Matola was aware that more than half of Belize was covered with tropical rain forest that harbored jaguars, tapirs, spider monkeys, and colorful birds. An impressive barrier reef edged its coastline. Although the government had placed almost a third of the country in national parks and nature preserves, thousands of citizens were rapidly stripping the rest of the land's natural resources. There seemed to be a need to educate the public about their environment.

In 1983, starting with the movie animals she had inherited, Matola set up a tiny zoo on the edge of the forest. Then, working tirelessly, she began to spread her conservation message to the people. Visiting schools, sending out newsletters, meeting with government officials, she gradually made her message clear: take care of natural habitats.

Today, the Belize Zoo is widely known, and the people of Belize are no longer indifferent to their environment. The government and wealthy citizens take wildlife into account when they make land-use decisions. One Belizean businessman has turned 4,000 acres of his land into a wildlife sanctuary, inspiring his neighbors to do the same. Another who owns more than 200,000 acres of jungle sold more than half of his land to a conservation group rather than to a large cattle company that would have turned the land into pasture.

Research and the frozen zoo

While people like Sharon Matola begin the conservation process in some countries, experts

Matola started the Belize Zoo in 1983 in hopes of convincing Belizeans to preserve the country's wilderness areas.

in other zoos work to save endangered animals by developing techniques that will make breeding easier and more reliable. Artificial insemination, introducing sperm into a female animal to produce offspring, is one such technique.

For decades, artificial insemination has been used regularly with domestic cattle and sheep. More recently it has been tried with rarer species such as gazelles, wolves, peregrine falcons, and golden eagles. Success has come slowly. An artificially inseminated gorilla successfully gave birth at the Royal Melbourne Zoological Gardens (Melbourne Zoo) in 1984. In 1992, the birth of two leopard-cat kittens from an artificially inseminated female marked one of the first times the process has been successful with exotic cats.

Artificial insemination promises to be especially useful for zoos that take part in Species Survival Plans. Shipping large animals such as Siberian tigers or Sumatran rhinos from one zoo to another for breeding is stressful for the animal and expensive for the zoo. Transporting a test tube containing the animal's sperm across country, however, is a painless process.

Artificial insemination will also eliminate other problems that may arise when animals are to mate. "You may buy a male rhino an air ticket and get him somewhere only to find that the female doesn't like him," points out Nate Flesness, executive director of ISIS, the computer database for zoo animals.

Sperm and egg banking

The process of artificial insemination goes hand in hand with another development known as sperm and egg banking. Researchers collect reproductive material—sperm and eggs—from animals, then fertilize the eggs in a test tube or petri dish in the lab. This process is called in vitro fertilization. In what is known as the frozen zoo, sperm and fertilized eggs are quick-frozen and stored in containers of liquid nitrogen for use at a later time. Frozen sperm can then be thawed and used for artificial insemination. A previously frozen egg can be implanted in a surrogate, a substitute mother, who will carry the baby until it is ready to be born.

Surrogacy is a third technique being tried by some zoo researchers. In an experiment at the Bronx Zoo in 1981, the fertilized egg of a gaur, a wild cow native to Asia, was implanted in a female Holstein cow named Flossie. Several months later, Flossie gave birth to a healthy gaur calf. At the Cincinnati Zoo in 1984, an eland (a large African antelope) gave birth to a bongo (a small African antelope) that had been implanted.

Sperm and fertilized eggs are quick-frozen and stored in containers of liquid nitrogen at the San Diego Zoo's Center for Reproduction of Endangered Species. The sperm is later thawed for artificial insemination; the eggs can be implanted in a surrogate mother.

The frozen skin cells of more than two hundred species of mammals provide a source of DNA and limitless possibilities for future research.

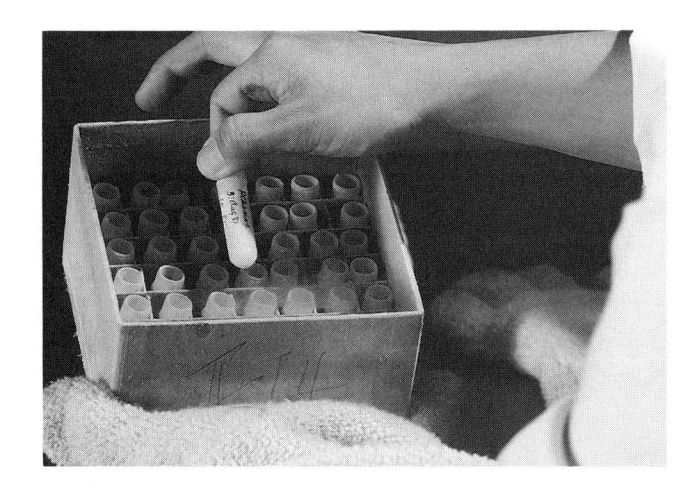

Researchers hope that using non-endangered animals as surrogate mothers for related endangered species will become a common practice in years to come.

Other technology also leads experts to dream of unlocking secrets of the past and making further breakthroughs in the future. Through the analysis of DNA (the genetic compound deoxyribonucleic acid) isolated from a preserved quagga skin, researchers have begun to find answers to their questions about this relation of the zebra that became extinct more than one hundred years ago. At the San Diego Zoo's Center for Reproduction of Endangered Species, frozen skin cells of two hundred species of mammals are kept as a source of DNA for possible future research. Extinct species may one day be reborn, using genetic material that has been preserved this way. Says Oliver Ryder, geneticist, "Future generations won't be happy about what has been lost, but they'll be thankful for what we save."

At what cost?

Artificial insemination, sperm and egg banking, and surrogacy are promising techniques for saving endangered animals. They are also expensive, adding to the already high costs of running a modern zoo.

From veterinary bills to food for the animals, everything costs money. In 1990, running the Bronx Zoo cost more than $22 million. The 1991 budget for the San Diego Zoo and its neighboring Wild Animal Park was more than $70 million.

A large percentage of that money is used to hire staff and to maintain zoo facilities. Some wonder if those funds would be better spent on preserving animals in the wild. Will Travers of Zoo Check, an animal rights organization based in Great Britain, points out that zoo experts spent more than $21.6 million to save the Arabian oryx. A similar amount went to the California condor project. Travers notes:

> When you add that to an annual global zoo budget of more than $865 million, the question cannot be avoided. What could that sort of money do for the conservation of natural habitat, the conservation of plants and animals in the habitat?

Money-raising techniques

That question leads to another. In a world of tight budgets and limited income, how do zoos raise the large sums of money they need to maintain these expensive programs? In the past, entry to zoos was free. Tax dollars supported many facilities across the country. Today, that support is disappearing, and directors rely on zoological societies, private donations, and ticket sales to meet zoo needs.

The new money-raising techniques seem to be working. The San Diego Zoo is one of many that depends on a strong zoological society for much of its income. It recorded 180,000 family memberships in 1990. Zoo Atlanta turned to local businesses and organizations when modernizing the zoo in the early 1990s. Pittsburgh and other

From research and maintenance to supplying huge quantities of food for the animals, it is becoming extremely expensive to run a zoo.

zoos are doing the same for a part of their revenue each year.

Although private donations are important, ticket sales bring in the bulk of funds in most modern zoos. In 1991, Zoo Atlanta estimated that entry fees made up almost one-half of its income. Once visitors are through the gate, money spent at snack bars and gift shops boosts the totals.

Zoos go to great lengths to ensure that ticket sales remain high. Well-designed habitat exhibits are a top priority. Their popularity with the public justifies the high cost and enormous effort it takes to create them. Recognizing that fact, in 1992 a group of businessmen, bankers, and developers proposed adding several new habitat exhibits to Regent's Park Zoo, in hopes of saving that struggling institution.

Many zoos have special in-park activities to bring in extra money. The Seattle Zoo hosts a series of summer concerts every year. Point Defiance Zoo in Tacoma, Washington, puts on Zoolights, a nighttime spectacular that draws thousands of visitors during the holiday season. In a controversial move, Metrozoo officials in Florida added paddle boats and a miniature golf course to draw repeat crowds. Some people complain that the additions have introduced an amusement park atmosphere to the facility.

Animal preserves

Because zoos are both costly and limited in size, other less expensive, more efficient ways of protecting endangered species may need to be developed. One of those possibilities is the national park, refuge, or preserve.

Several of these large parcels of land already exist today, set aside so that animals can roam and multiply in their native environments. Unlike their relatives in conservation centers, animals in

To keep public interest and ticket sales high, many zoos work hard and spend a lot of money on the design of their exhibits.

Animals live in their natural environments in Florida's Everglades National Park. National parks and animal preserves play an important role in the protection of endangered species.

these preserves find food and shelter for themselves. They cope unaided with illness and predators. They are, for the most part, left alone by humans to survive in the wild.

In China, the recently formed Qian Tang Reserve may be the largest animal preserve in the world, covering 100,000 square miles and protecting yak (long-haired wild oxen), snow leopards, and Tibetan brown bears. In Tanzania and South Africa, zebras, lions, and other native species live within the boundaries of Serengeti National Park and Kruger National Park, two world-famous preserves.

In the United States, Everglades National Park harbors crocodiles, manatees (whalelike mammals), and most of the dwindling population of Florida panthers. In Yellowstone National Park, 120,000 bison roam in safety, although park officials cull some of their animals if the herd gets too large.

The legitimate game ranch

The game ranch may be another alternative to zoos in the future. On legitimate ranches, those that do not promote canned hunts, owners preserve endangered wildlife while they legally raise game animals for meat or for sport hunting.

Many conservationists find the purposes of these ranches contradictory and unacceptable. They flinch at the idea of killing wild animals, especially exotic animals such as rhinos or kudos (large antelope) that can be found on African ranches. But other wildlife biologists see advantages to this system. First, because true sportspeople prefer hunting in a natural environment, great effort is made to preserve habitats. Trees, bushes, and grasslands are untouched. In Africa, this is especially important, given that many landowners would otherwise turn to farming or cattle ranching, which destroys habitats.

Secondly, only certain species are killed. Countless others, such as monkeys, birds, and insects, are not hunted and can safely live in these protected areas.

Finally, ranchers who make profits by raising game animals are interested in conserving those species. Hunters may kill a few animals, but the majority survive. Says wildlife researcher Rob Little, "Let the species become of value rather than drawing (subsidized) funds out of society. In that way wildlife will automatically prosper."

Weaknesses

In Africa, private ownership of native wildlife has helped reestablish habitats for many threatened species. Within the boundaries of game ranches and preserves, populations of wild animals are on the rise. However, for preserves and game ranches to reach their full potential in the future, several weaknesses have to be addressed.

Elk ranchers in Canada have discovered that outbreaks of tuberculosis can all but wipe out a herd. Disease can easily spread to domestic cattle and other wild animals. In one 1990 Canadian epidemic, more than four hundred animals, including moose, deer, yak, and wild boar, had to be destroyed.

Experts predict other crises will arise as well. "The animals have been placed in a zoo—a big zoo," warns William Conway. "Inbreeding will be a problem. Zoo-like techniques will have to take place."

Llanos of South America

A less controversial alternative to zoos already exists in Venezuela on the grassy savannas known as llanos. There, ranchers have struck a unique compromise with nature.

Ranches on the llanos can be enormous, reaching up to 160,000 acres. Some of the land is used for grazing; 5 million of the 6.4 million of Venezuela's cattle are bred in this area. But cattle also share territory with wild animals native to

A herd of elephants wanders through Kenya's Amboseli National Park. Wildlife populations in such animal preserves are on the rise.

Whether they are called bioparks, conservation centers, or some other name, modern zoos are pleasing the public as never before.

the region: howler monkeys, jaguars, capybaras (pig-sized rodents), and anteaters, to name a few.

Unlike the owners of private ranches in Africa, many ranchers in the llanos have forbidden the hunting of wild creatures on their properties. "Big ranchers can afford to support the survival of wildlife, even predators—they don't mind losing a few calves to jaguars," explains John Eisenberg, zoologist.

Researchers and other naturalists who frequently visit the llanos are careful to protect the natural habitat that is increasingly hard to find in a world of shrinking wilderness. "Mammals, reptiles, amphibians, large and easily visible flocks of birds—they're all here," says one American who regularly leads bird-watching tours.

Conservationists are hopeful that nearby countries with similar savannas—Colombia, Brazil, and Bolivia—will soon follow Venezuela's lead and act to preserve wildlife before the losses become too great.

Bioparks

Such easy compromises between humans and nature are unusual today. Some people are greedy, thoughtless, or ignorant. Others are poor. They cannot always place the welfare of animals before their own.

Zoos can be a reminder of the need for compromise. But many zoo directors now believe that the traditional word "zoo" no longer expresses their more serious purpose. Some are convinced that a new title is needed to reflect the changes that are being made.

The NYZS/Wildlife Conservation Society is leading the way. In 1993 the society substituted the words "wildlife conservation park" for "zoo" in the titles of its five animal facilities. The change has raised some dispute, yet members of the society hope that people will begin to accept the new name as they better understand the zoo's changing responsibilities.

Michael Robinson of the National Zoo believes that zoos of the future should be called "bioparks" rather than wildlife centers. Robinson hopes that the name will emphasize the need to preserve entire ecosystems, including plants, animals, water, and air. In his words:

> Zoos are . . . powerful forces of biological education, places where people can be moved by the wonder and glory of real living things to act to save ecosystems rather than species. Species saving is valuable for a handful of irreplaceable masterpieces, but we must save the Gallery of Life on earth, not just some of the paintings.

Whether they are known as bioparks, conservation centers, or by some other name, today's well-managed zoos are far different from those of the past. Some people may continue to believe that keeping animals in captivity is wrong, that zoos are too expensive to maintain, and that zoo goals are too optimistic to become reality. Nevertheless, the modern zoo is pleasing the public as never before. Unless public mood changes, zoos are here to stay.

If they stay, they will continue to improve. Zoos are taking their responsibilities as nature's protectors seriously. They are responding to demands of an ever-changing world. They are looking ahead and preparing for the challenges of tomorrow.

Glossary

anthropomorphism: The practice of attributing human qualities to animals or nonliving things.

artificial insemination: The process of artificially introducing male genetic material (sperm) into a female to produce offspring.

biopark: A combination of zoo and botanical garden that may display entire ecosystems; a possible alternative to zoos in the future.

breed: a) n. a kind or type; b) v. to bring forth offspring; to reproduce.

charismatic megavertebrate: A large, exotic animal such as an elephant, tiger, zebra, or giraffe, traditionally exhibited in zoos because of its popularity with visitors.

conservation: The care and protection of natural resources, such as forests, water, or animals.

culling: The practice of humanely killing surplus zoo animals.

curator: Zoo worker who oversees species and helps set policy for the zoo. A curator is often responsible for creating exhibits and deciding which animals should be bred.

demography: Science dealing with populations, their distribution, density, growth, and so forth.

deoxyribonucleic acid (DNA): Genetic material responsible for inherited traits, found in the nuclei of all cells.

ecology: Science that deals with relationships between living organisms and their environment.

ecosystem: The most complex level of organization in

nature, made up of animals, plants, and bacteria, and their relationships with each other and the environment. An ecosystem also includes climate, soil, water, and energy.

endangered species: Groups of plants or animals in danger of becoming extinct.

environment: All the conditions that surround and affect living organisms, including weather, food supply, and other living organisms.

environmentalist: Person working to solve environmental problems, such as air and water pollution.

flight distance: Distance within which an animal allows an enemy to approach before it tries to escape.

genetic diversity: Condition in which a population has a variety of genetic forms, such as genes for various eye colors. With a loss of genetic diversity, populations are less able to adapt to changes in their environment.

genetics: Branch of biology that deals with heredity, the passing of characteristics from parents to their offspring.

habitat: Region in which a plant or animal lives.

imprinting: A learning process, occurring in very young animals, in which they recognize the first moving object they see as a parent or role model. Animals that imprint on animals of another species may never learn to recognize members of their own species.

inbreeding: The too-frequent mating of closely related individuals, resulting in loss of genetic diversity.

in vitro: Artificially maintained, such as in a test tube or petri dish.

keeper: Primary caretaker of zoo animals, responsible for cleaning cages, feeding animals, and maintaining records of behavior.

llanos: Level, grassy plains covering large areas in South America.

menagerie: A collection of wild animals kept in cages or enclosures for exhibition purposes.

naturalist: Person who studies nature.

nocturnal: Active during the night.

poacher: Person who hunts or catches animals illegally, especially by trespassing.

propagate: To cause a plant or animal to reproduce; to raise or breed.

reintroduction: The process of returning zoo animals to a habitat similar to that from which their species originated.

reserve: Land set apart for a special purpose.

sanctuary: A reservation where animals or birds are protected.

species: A group of animals that shares similar characteristics and the ability to produce fertile offspring.

speciesism: Term describing discrimination against animals; based on the belief that some animals have more worth than others, and that all are inferior to human beings.

Species Survival Plan: A program whose goal is to rebuild populations of endangered species; established about 1980 by the American Zoo and Aquarium Association.

surrogate: A substitute.

threatened species: Groups of plants or animals that are disappearing and may soon become endangered.

vandalism: Mischievous, intentional destruction of property.

zoologist: A specialist in zoology, that branch of biology that deals with animals, their life, growth, classification, and so forth.

Organizations to Contact

The following organizations provide information about zoos, endangered species, and animal welfare. For further information about zoos, contact a zoo in your local area.

American Zoo and Aquarium Association (AZA)
7970-D Old Georgetown Rd.
Bethesda, MD 20814
(301) 907-7777

AZA is an association of North American zoos and aquariums. The organization is instrumental in coordinating breeding programs for endangered species. Brochures on its activities are available.

The Humane Society of the United States (HSUS)
2100 L St. NW
Washington, DC 20037
(202) 452-1100

HSUS works for "the protection of all animals—pets, wildlife, farm and entertainment animals—through educational, legislative, investigative and legal means." The society issues a quarterly magazine, *The HSUS News*, as well as *KIND Teacher* and *KIND News*, publications for elementary school teachers and students. The society offers a catalog of posters, bumper stickers, books, filmstrips, fact sheets, and reprints.

Minnesota Zoo Discovery Program
13000 Zoo Blvd.
Apple Valley, MN 55124
(612) 431-9234

The Discovery Program offers fact sheets regarding specific animals at the Minnesota Zoo, as well as brochures regarding zoo careers. Written requests are preferred. The zoo provides a variety of educational programs, including literature and books about endangered animals.

National Zoological Park
3001 Connecticut Ave. NW
Washington, DC 20077
(202) 357-1300 or (202) 673-4800

The National Zoo offers a variety of wildlife education programs for children and adults. Its publications include newsletters, plus information on the zoo's Conservation and Research Center and its Center for New Opportunities in Animal Health, where scientists work to save endangered species using artificial reproduction. The zoo also provides information on its Wildlife Nutrition Program, carried out through the Center for Biological Research.

New York Zoological Society/Wildlife Conservation Society
Bronx Zoo
Bronx, NY 10460
(718) 220-5131 or (718) 220-5100

The motto of the society is "Conservation, Education, and Science." It publishes animal fact sheets, newsletters, and other brochures. A branch of the society, Friends of Wildlife Conservation, provides answers to questions about specific endangered animals. The Bronx Zoo offers a variety of educational programs for children and adults.

People for the Ethical Treatment of Animals (PETA)
PO Box 42516
Washington, DC 20015
(301) 770-7444

PETA works to protect the rights of animals "through public education, research and investigations, legislation, special events, direct action and grassroots organizing." The organization publishes *PETA News*, as well as guidelines on ways to make the world a better place for animals. PETA offers a catalog of publications, videos, buttons, bumper stickers, clothing, and cruelty-free products.

San Diego Zoo Education Department
PO Box 551
San Diego, CA 92112
(619) 231-1515

The zoo's Education Department provides fact sheets regarding specific animals at the San Diego Zoo and San Diego Wild Animal Park. The department offers brochures regarding zoo careers. All requests must be in writing. The zoo and park schedule a variety of educational programs for children and adults.

Suggestions for Further Reading

Joyce Altman and Sue Goldberg, *Dear Bronx Zoo*. New York: Macmillan, 1990.

Ginny Johnston and Jody Cutchins, *Windows on Wildlife*. New York: Morrow Junior Books, 1990.

Tim O'Brien, *Where the Animals Are: A Guide to the Best Zoos, Aquariums, and Wildlife Sanctuaries in North America*. Old Saybrook, CT: The Globe Pequot Press, 1992.

Terry O'Neill, *Zoos*. San Diego, CA: Greenhaven Press, 1990.

Wendy Pfeffer, *Popcorn Park Zoo*. Englewood Cliffs, NJ: Julian Messner (Simon and Schuster), 1992.

Peggy Thomson, *Keepers and Creatures at the National Zoo*. New York: Thomas Y. Crowell, 1988.

Works Consulted

The Animals' Agenda, "Zoos and Aquariums,." April 1992, May 1992, June 1992, July/August 1992.

Tom Arrandale, "A New Breed of Zoo," *Sierra*, November/December 1990.

Peter Batten, *Living Trophies*. New York: Thomas Y. Crowell, 1976.

Robert Bendiner, *The Fall of the Wild, The Rise of the Zoo*. New York: E.P. Dutton, 1981.

Jesse Birnbaum, "Just Too Beastly for Words," *Time*, June 24, 1991.

Chris Bolgiano, "The Fall of the Wild," *Wilderness*, Spring 1992.

Russell Bourne, ed., *A Zoo for All Seasons*. Washington, DC: Smithsonian Exposition Books (distributed by W.W. Norton, New York), 1979.

Diane Brady, "Animal Farms," *Maclean's*, May 10, 1993.

Bill Bruns, *A World of Animals*. New York: Harry N. Abrams, 1983.

John F. Burns, "At Sarajevo Zoo, the Last Survivor Dies," *The New York Times*, November 4, 1992.

Betsy Carpenter, "Upsetting the Ark," *U.S. News & World Report*, August 24, 1992.

Merritt Clifton, "Chucking Zoo Animals Overboard," *The Animals' Agenda*, March 1988.

———, "Killing the Captives," *The Animals' Agenda*, September 1991.

———, "'Low-Class, No-Class Slime Balls': Zoo Official," *The Animals' Agenda*, December 1991.

———, "Wanted: Wildlife—Dead or Alive," *The Animals' Agenda*, June 1991.

Francis X. Clines, "What's 3 Letters and Zoologically Incorrect?" *The New York Times*, February 4, 1993.

Jeffrey P. Cohn, "Decisions at the Zoo," *BioScience*, October 1992.

Martine Collette, "Lions and Tigers and Hummingbirds, Oh My!" *Los Angeles*, January 1990.

Nicholas Dawidoff, "Like Sardines in the Can," *Sports Illustrated*, October 29, 1990.

———, "Queen of the Jungle," *Sports Illustrated*, March 9, 1992.

Shawn Doherty, "The Scandal of Atlanta's Zoo," *Newsweek*, June 18, 1984.

The Economist, "Save the Zoo," January 11, 1992.

James Fisher, *Zoos of the World*. Garden City, NY: The American Museum of Natural History, 1967.

Dan Fost, "Zoo Marketers Stalk Human Targets," *American Demographics*, October 1991.

Nancy Gibbs, "A New Zoo: A Modern Ark," *Time*, August 21, 1989.

Eric Hoffman, "Wonder Woman of Belize," *International Wildlife*, November/December 1992.

International Wildlife, "Chinese Take Steps to Save River Dolphin," January/February 1993.

———, "New Strides in Captive Breeding of Rare Cats," August/September 1992.

Jonathan Kandell, "In a Land of Capybaras and Cattle," *Audubon*, September/October 1992.

David M. Kennedy, "What's New at the Zoo?" *Technology Review*, April 1987.

Marcia King, "Asphalt 'Jungles,'" *The Animals' Agenda*, July/August 1992.

Gini Kopecky, "Free Willy . . . And Maybe Rescue Keiko, Too," *The New York Times*, July 11, 1993.

Jon R. Luoma, "Back Home on the Range?" *Audubon*, March/April 1993.

———, "Born to Be Wild," *Audubon*, January/February 1992.

———, *The Crowded Ark*. Boston: Houghton Mifflin, 1987.

———, "Saving the Popular Giant Panda from Being Loved to Death," *The New York Times*, April 27, 1993.

John Maddox, "Non-Profit Profits from Animals," *Nature*, February 7, 1991.

Steven Manning, "Life in the Balance," *Scholastic Update*, April 16, 1993.

Emily Mitchell, "Shooting Leopards in a Barrel," *Time*, June 10, 1991.

New Scientist, "Brussels Wages War on 'Prison Zoos,'" July 20, 1991.

Tim O'Brien, *Where the Animals Are*. Old Saybrook, CT: The Globe Pequot Press, 1992.

Patricia Orwen, "The Roar About Zoos," *World Press Review*, July 1991.

Jake Page, *Zoo, The Modern Ark*. New York: Facts on File, 1990.

Tom Pawlick, "Operation Booger Man," *National Wildlife*, August/September 1991.

Karen N. Peart, "What a Zoo! (Or Whatever . . .)," *Scholastic Update*, April 16, 1993.

Michael H. Robinson, "The Age of the Biopark," *The World & I*, September 1993.

Karen F. Schmidt, "Preserving the Genetic Legacies," *U.S. News & World Report*, August 24, 1992.

William E. Schmidt, "$1.85 Million from Kuwait Emir

Saves London Zoo, for Now," *The New York Times*, June 25, 1992.

Serving Time (video). Canadian Broadcasting Corp., 1987.

Charles Siebert, "Where Have All the Animals Gone?" *Harper's Magazine*, May 1991.

Ed Struzik, "Trouble Back at the Game Ranch," *International Wildlife*, July/August 1992.

Chriss Swaney, "New Zoo Director on Safari to Capture More City Visitors," *Pittsburgh Business Times*, July 23, 1990.

Cliff Tarpy, "New Zoos—Taking Down the Bars," *National Geographic*, July 1993.

Time, "Lied Jungle, Henry Doorly Zoo, Omaha, Nebraska," January 4, 1993.

Colin Tudge, "Good Breeding Doesn't Always Show," *New Scientist*, February 17, 1990.

———, *Last Animals at the Zoo*. Washington, DC: Island Press, 1992.

Robert Wade, ed., *Wild in the City*. San Diego: A San Diego Zoo/Wild Animal Park Publication, 1985.

David Walls, *The Activists Almanac*. New York: Simon and Schuster, 1993.

Stephen Weaver, "The Elephant's Best Friend," *National Review*, August 12, 1991.

Mary Welch, "Lion's Share of Zoo Funds Going Private," *Atlanta Business Chronicle*, April 22, 1991.

Ted Williams, "Canned Hunts," *Audubon*, January/February 1992.

Lord Zuckerman, "The Zoo That Has to Close," *Nature*, June 25, 1992.

Katherine Zwerin, "Zoos: A Blueprint for Fiscal Survival," *Parks and Recreation*, March 1986.

Index

addaxes, 87
Africa
  animal preserves in, 103
  game ranches in, 104, 106
Akbar, 13, 14
Alligator River National Wildlife Refuge, 92
American Zoo and Aquarium Association (AZA), 53-54, 62, 70, 71, 83
animal baiting, 14
animal preserves, 102-103
  problems in, 104-105
animals
  artificial insemination of, 98-99
  behavioral needs of, 35, 39
  boredom of, 21, 33, 50
  breeding of
    birth control and, 89-90
    captive-bred, 62
    cheetahs, 13-14, 83, 88
    inbreeding dangers of, 82-83
    loans for, 85
    overcrowding and, 60, 70-75
    studies on, 42-43
    tamarins, 37-39
  canned hunts of, 71, 104
  collecting of, 11, 15, 23, 60-62
    regulations and, 61
  comfortable space for, 28-29
  cruelty to
    laws against, 21, 54-55
  diets of, 36-37
    mistreatment and, 8, 51
  disease and, 41-42, 51, 104-105
  early housing of, 20-21, 27
  endangered
    Bengal tiger, 65, 73
    efforts to protect, 80-93, 99-100
    giant panda, 53-54, 65
    gnatcatcher, 65
    in natural environment, 55
    regulations covering, 54, 61-62, 80
    zoos and, 7, 54, 60, 77, 81-93

extinction of, 65-67, 77-78
feeding of, 8, 35
flight distance of, 29
killed for sport, 65, 71, 103-106
mating habits of, 88-89
mistreatment of 8, 21-22, 27, 46-53, 57
  historically, 13-14, 20-21
natural habitats of destroyed, 65, 77, 78, 79
New World discoveries of, 15-17
performing, 34-35
psychological and social needs of, 33-34, 38-39, 50-52
release of into the wild, 73-74, 90-93
see also individual animals
Animals' Agenda, The, 48, 50
anteaters, 32
antelopes, 24, 88
apes, 12, 41
Aristotle, 13
Arizona-Sonora Museum, 32
armadillos, 16
Arnett, Johnny, 65
artificial insemination, 98-99
Ashurbanipal, 12
Asia
  historical zoos in, 12-13
  Shanghai Zoo, 73
Audubon Society, The, 22
auk, great, 78
Australia
  zoos in, 32-33, 99
Austria
  Schönbrunn Zoo, 17
aviaries
  historical, 12, 15-16, 17, 29, 82
  restyled, 29
Aztecs
  zoos and, 15-16

baboons, 39
Baltimore Children's Zoo, 69
Banks, Sir Joseph, 19

Bartholomew, Charles, 71
bats, 30, 31
Batten, Peter, 52
bears
  activities of, 35
  in historical zoos, 13, 16, 25
  Kodiak, 47
  Malayan sun, 30
  polar, 47
  sloth, 35-36
  Tibetan brown, 103
Belize Zoo, 95-97
Berlin Zoo, 18, 20
Bertsch, Amy, 63
Bevan, Laura, 51
birds
  aviaries, 12, 15-16, 17, 29, 82
  extinction of, 78
  habitat exhibits, 31
breeding of zoo animals, 62
  birth control and, 89-90
  cheetahs, 13-14, 83, 88
  dangers of inbreeding, 82-83
  loans for, 85
  overcrowding and, 60, 70-75
  studies on, 42-43
  tamarins, 37-39
Bring 'Em Back Alive (Buck), 60
Bronx Zoo, 7-8, 19, 33, 99, 101
Buck, Frank, 60-61
Buffalo (NY) Zoo, 19

camels, 12, 20
Canada
  animal disease outbreaks in, 104-105
  zoos in, 56, 57
canned hunts, 71, 104
Carl Hagenbeck Tierpark, 24
Central America
  Belize Zoo, 95-97
  historical zoos in, 15-16
Central Park Wildlife Conservation Center, 19, 52
cheetahs
  breeding of in zoos, 13-14, 83, 88
  historical zoos and, 12, 13-14
chimpanzees
  historical zoos and, 12, 14
  human diseases and, 14
  performing by, 34
  stress behavior of, 51
  trading of, 82
China
  animal preserves in, 103
Chisholm, Ken, 74

Cincinnati Zoo, 75
  breeding at, 83, 88-89, 99
  conservation center supported by, 87
  Insect World exhibit, 82
Cleveland Zoo, 87
  Creatures of the Night exhibit, 32
Columbus, Christopher
  New World animals and, 15
Columbus (OH) Zoological Gardens, 45, 53, 69, 87
condors
  in Louis XIII's zoo, 17
  release of to the wild, 92-93, 101
conservation centers, 86-88, 102
  Central Park Wildlife Conservation Center, 19, 52
  Devonian Wildlife Conservation Centre, 88
  International Wildlife Conservation Park, 7-8, 19
  Jersey Wildlife Preservation Trust, 67
  National Zoo's Conservation and Research Center, 87, 89
  New York Zoo's Rare Animal Survival Center, 87
  Whipsnade Wildlife Park, 88
  Wilds, the, 87
Convention on International Trade in Endangered Species (CITES), 54, 61
Conway, William
  on culling animals, 72
  on education programs, 67
  on game preserves, 105
  on help for endangered species, 78, 80, 93
Cortés, Hernando, 15-16
cougars, 16, 20
cranes, sandhill, 89
crocodiles, 14, 29
Crowded Ark, The (Luoma), 45, 73
culling, 70, 72-73

deer
  in King Solomon's zoo, 12
  Pére David's, 66-67
Devonian Wildlife Conservation Centre, 88
DNA research, 100
dodo, 78
du Bois, Thaya, 35
Düsseldorf Zoo, 20

eagles, 99

education
  zoo programs and, 7, 8, 45, 67-69
  historical, 13
Eisenberg, John, 106
elephants
  capture of, 23
  diet of, 37
  historical zoos and, 12, 13, 14, 20, 21
  mistreatment of, 8, 47
  rides on, 28, 48
  social behavior of, 8
emus, 17
endangered animals
  Bengal tiger, 65, 73
  efforts to protect, 80-93, 99-100
  giant panda, 53-54, 65
  gnatcatcher, 65
  in natural environment, 55
  regulations covering, 54, 61-62, 80
  zoos and, 7, 54, 60, 77-78, 81-93
Endangered Species Act, 61-62, 80
England
  historical zoos in, 19, 20-21, 25
  London Zoo, 88
  Regent's Park Zoo, 18-20, 25, 47-48, 102
  Zoological Society of London, 19, 48
Everglades National Park, 103
extinction of animals, 65-67, 77-78

falcons
  artificial insemination of, 99
  historical zoos and, 13
Federal Animal Welfare Act, 54, 56
ferrets, 92
fish, 16
Flesness, Nate, 98
France
  historical zoos in, 16-18
Francis I, Emperor, 17
Frederick William IV, King, 18
Free Willy (movie), 49-50

game ranches
  African, 104, 106
  legitimate, 103-104
  problems in, 71, 104-105
  South American, 105-106
gazelles
  artificial insemination of, 99
  habitat exhibits for, 31, 87
  historical zoos and, 24
  social behavior of, 39
Germany
  historical zoos in, 18, 20, 22-24
gibbons, 39
giraffes
  habitat exhibits for, 31
  historical zoos and, 11-12, 14, 27, 61
gnatchatcher, as endangered, 65
goats, 25
gorillas
  artificial insemination of, 98
  illegally captured, 62
  mistreatment of, 47, 49, 57
Grandy, John, 70
Grant Park Zoo
  problems in, 46-47, 57
Great Smoky Mountain National Park, 92
Greeks
  zoos for eduction and, 13
Greenpeace, 80
guinea pigs, 17

Hagenbeck, Carl, 22-25, 27, 60
Hanna, Jack, 45, 69
Hatshepsut, Queen, 11
hawks, 13
Hediger, Heine, 29, 33-34, 40
Henry Doorly Zoo, Lied Jungle exhibit, 30
Hilker, Cathryn, 75
hippos
  habitat exhibits for, 30, 31
  historical zoos and, 13, 14
History of Animals (Aristotle), 13
horses, 12
Humane Society of the United States, 21, 51, 70
hyraxes, 31

insects, 80, 82
in vitro fertilization, 98-99
International Species Information System (ISIS), 84, 98
International Union for the Conservation of Nature and Natural Resources (IUCN), 80
International Wildlife Conservation Park, 7-8, 19

jaguars, 16
Jersey Wildlife Preservation Trust, 67
Joseph II, Emperor, 17

Kaiser, Sandra, 9
kangaroos, 17

Keiko, orca whale, 49-50
King, Marcia, 50
klipspringers, 31
koalas, 33
Krantz, Palmer, 27
Kruger National Park, 103
Kublai Khan, 13
kudos, 104

Landres, Lisa, 52, 56
langurs, 62
Lecky, W.E.H., 14
lemurs, 17, 35, 81
leopards, 99, 103
Lied Jungle exhibit, 30
Lincoln Park Zoo, 19
lions
  historical zoos and, 12-14, 20, 21, 24
  mating habits of, 88
Little, Rob, 104
lizards, 31
llamas, 17
llanos, as preserves, 105-106
London Zoo, 88
loris, slow, 39-40
Los Angeles Zoo, 35
Louis XIII, King, 16-17
Luoma, Jon, 45, 73, 77

Mackintosh, Michael, 57
maleos, 89
manatees, 103
Mann, William M., 61
Marco Polo, 13
marmosets, 82
Matola, Sharon, 95-97
McBain, Jim, 50
Metro Toronto Zoo, 65
Metrozoo, 102
Middle East
  historical zoos in, 11-12
Minnesota Zoological Gardens, 35-36, 67, 73, 84
monkeys
  activities of, 29, 35
  capture of, 23
  habitat exhibits for, 29, 30, 31
  historical zoos and, 13, 17, 20, 27
  social needs of, 33-34
Montali, Richard, 41
Montezuma, 16
Moscow Zoo, 51-52

National Zoo (National Zoological Park), 45, 107
  animal collecting and, 61
  animal diets and, 36
  Conservation and Research Center, 87, 89
  disease control at, 41-42
  endangered species and, 82
  established, 19-20
  study on inbreeding, 83
  tamarin research at, 38, 91
Nature Conservancy, The, 80
Nebuchadnezzar, 12
New York Zoological Society, Rare Animal Survival Center, 87
Newkirk, Ingrid, 64
Noah's ark, 11
NYZS/Wildlife Conservation Society
  William Conway and, 72, 80
  members of, 7, 47
  worldwide projects of, 67
  zoo names and, 106-107

opossum, Leadbeater's, 33
orangutans
  hybrid, 86
  illegally captured, 62
  performing by, 34
oryx, 91, 101
ostriches, 12

panda, giant
  as endangered, 53-54, 65
  diet of, 37
  historical zoos and, 13
panda, lesser, 82
panthers, 103
parrots, 12, 30, 62
peacocks, 12
penguins, 17, 31
People for the Ethical Treatment of Animals (PETA), 63, 64
Pére David's deer, 66-67
pheasants, 12
Philadelphia Zoological Society, 19, 82
Phillips, David, 9
Phoenix Zoo, 91
Pichner, Jim, 36
pigeons, passenger, 78
Pittsburgh Zoo, 102
platypus, 33
Poco das Antes rain forest reserve, 91
Point Defiance Zoo, 68, 102
Polito's Royal Menagerie, 20
porcupines, 13, 32

Prospect Park Zoo, 47
Przewalski's horses, 67
Ptolemy II, King, 12, 14
Puerto Rican crested toads, 92

Qian Tang Reserve, 103

raccoons, 17
Raffles, Sir Thomas Stamford, 19
Ramses II, King, 12
Rare Animal Survival Center, 87, 89
Red Data Book, 80
Regent's Park Zoo
  buildings, 18, 20
  founding of, 19
  habitat exhibits at, 102
  Mappin Terraces exhibit, 25
  problems in, 47-48
rhinoceros
  capture of, 23
  game farms and, 104
  historical zoos and, 12, 13, 14
  mating habits of, 88
Riverbanks Zoo, 27
Robinson, Michael, 107
Roman Empire, zoos in, 14
Royal Melbourne Zoological
  Gardens, 99
royal zoos, 11-14, 16-18
Ryder, Oliver, 100

San Diego Wild Animal Park, 87, 92, 101
San Diego Zoo, 45
  African Rock Kopje exhibit, 31
  Center for Reproduction of
    Endangered Species, 100
  costs and fund-raising of, 101
  Harry Wegeforth and, 53
  Malayan sun bears exhibit, 30
  reintroduction programs, 91
  Wild Animal Park and, 87
San Jose Zoological Gardens, 52
sandhill cranes, 89
Schaller, George, 95
Schönbrunn Zoo, 17
sea lions, 34
Seal, Ulysses S., 84
Seattle Zoo, 102
Sea World, 50
  Penguin Encounter exhibit, 31-32
Serengeti National Park, 103
Sespe Condor Sanctuary, 93
Shanghai Zoo, 73
sheep, 20, 25
Sierra Club, 80

Slater Park Zoo, 8, 45
sloth bears, 35-36
sloths, 16
Smithsonian Institution, 20
snakes
  habitat exhibits for, 32
  historical zoos and, 12, 14, 16
Societies for the Prevention of
  Cruelty to Animals, 21
Society for Conservation Biology, 86
Solomon, King, 12
Soule, Michael, 86
South American animal preserves, 105-106
speciesism, 63-65
Species Survival Plans (SSPs), 83-86, 98
sperm and egg banking, 98-99
St. Louis Zoological Gardens, 25
Stanley Park Zoological Gardens, 57
Stellar's sea cow, 78
Styles, Toby, 65
surrogate mothers, animal, 99
Switzerland
  zoos in, 29

tamarins, golden lion,
  diet and, 37-38
  release to wild, 91-92
tapirs, 17, 30, 62
Taronga Zoo, 32-33
Tenochtitlán, 15-16
Texoma Hunting Wilderness, 71
tigers
  Bengal, 65, 73
  historical zoos and, 13, 14, 20, 21
  Javan, 78-79
  white, 83, 86
Toledo Zoo, 87
tortoises, 31
Travers, Will, 101
tropical rain forests
  destruction of, 79-80
  Poco das Antes rain forest reserve, 91
turkeys, 17
turtles, 16

Ujung Kulon National Park, 67
United States
  animal preserves in, 103
  first zoos in, 19-20
  Humane Society of, 21, 51, 70
  traveling and roadside zoos in, 48
  zoo regulatory agencies in, 53-56

see also individual zoos

veterinarians
  historical zoos and, 13, 16
  lack of, 51
  responsibilities of, 41-42

Wegeforth, Harry, 53
Wen Wang, Emperor, 12
whales, 49-50
Whipsnade Wildlife Park, 48, 88
Wilds, the, 87
wolves
  artificial insemination of, 99
  release to the wild of, 91, 92
  social behavior of, 39
Woodland Park Zoo
  African Savanna exhibit, 31
  Tropical/Nocturnal House, 32, 68
World Wildlife Fund, 80

yak, 103
Yellowstone National Park, 103

zebras
  habitat exhibits of, 31
  historical zoos and, 20, 24, 27
Zoo Atlanta, 46, 49, 69, 101, 102
Zoo Check, 101
zoo curators, 41
zoo directors, 40
zookeepers, 41
zoological societies, 19, 48
Zoological Society of London, 19, 48
Zoologischer Garten (Zurich Zoo), 29
Zoologischer Garten Berlin, 18, 20

zoos
  alternatives to, 86-88, 102-106
  animal welfare in, 23-25, 28
  as artificial, 59
  as cruel and unnecessary, 63
  as educational, 7, 8, 45, 67-69
  as entertainment, 7, 9, 14, 20
  as sanctuaries, 7, 59-60, 65-67, 75, 80-82
  benefits of, 66
  costs of running, 101
  early, animal housing in, 20-21, 27
  entry fees, 102
  favorite animals in, 81
  focusing collections, 81-82
  frozen, 98-99
  fund-raising for, 101-102
  historical, 11-25
  laws and regulations for, 21, 54-56
  mistreatment of animals in, 8, 13-14, 21-22, 27, 46-53
  natural habitats and, 7-9, 13-14, 23-25, 30
  opposition to, 8-9
  overcrowding in, 45, 52, 60, 70-75
  poorly run, 8, 45-53
  preservation projects of, 67, 96-98
  purpose of, 7, 59-60, 95
  roadside
    problems in, 47-49, 53
    regulatory agencies and, 55-56
  supervisory agencies and, 53-56
  surplus animals in, 70-75
  traveling, 20-21
    problems in, 47-49, 52-53
    regulatory agencies and, 55-56
  violence to animals in, 47, 51-52

About the Author

Diane Yancey began writing for her own entertainment when she was a thirteen-year-old living in Grass Valley, California. Later she graduated from Augustana College in Illinois. She now pursues a writing career in the Pacific Northwest, where she lives with her husband, two daughters, and two cats. Her interests include collecting old books, building miniature houses, and traveling.

Ms. Yancey's books include *Desperadoes and Dynamite*, *The Reunification of Germany*, *The Hunt for Hidden Killers*, and a book on the U.S. Camel Corps.

Picture Credits

Cover photo by Richard B. Levine
AP/Wide World Photos, 36, 52, 60, 63, 67, 84, 88, 105
© Nathan Benn/Woodfin Camp & Associates, Inc., 40, 64, 93
The Bettmann Archive, 17
© Ira Block/Woodfin Camp & Associates, Inc., 76
Margarite Bradley/Positive Images, 55
Department of Fish and Game, 70
Michael H. Francis, 103
© Kenneth Garrett/Woodfin Camp & Associates, Inc., 37, 87, 89, 100, 101
Luther C. Goldman, U.S. Fish & Wildlife Service, 78
© Michael Heron/Woodfin Camp & Associates, Inc., 66
Jerry Howard/Positive Images, 6, 8, 26, 32, 33, 34, 46, 50, 56, 69, 74, 81, 94, 102, 106
© Karen Kasmauski/Woodfin Camp & Associates, Inc., 99
© Richard B. Levine, 9, 58
Minnesota Zoo, 62, 72
National Zoological Park, Smithsonian Institution, 21
North Wind Picture Archives, 10, 16
Omaha's Henry Doorly Zoo, 30, 82
Photofest, 49
Point Defiance Zoo and Aquarium, 68
© Alon Reininger/ Woodfin Camp & Associates, Inc., 54
Reuters/Bettmann, 47, 90
Kevin Schafer/Sports Illustrated, 96, 97
D. Shane, World Wildlife Fund-U.S., 79
Stock Montage, Inc., 12, 13, 15, 18, 22, 23, 24
UPI/Bettmann, 28, 38, 42, 44, 61
Woodland Park Zoological Gardens, 31, 39
© Ian Yeomans/Woodfin Camp & Associates, Inc., 92